Mary Willcox Brown

The Development of Thrift

Mary Willcox Brown

The Development of Thrift

ISBN/EAN: 9783742810885

Manufactured in Europe, USA, Canada, Australia, Japa

Cover: Foto ©Andreas Hilbeck / pixelio.de

Manufactured and distributed by brebook publishing software
(www.brebook.com)

Mary Willcox Brown

The Development of Thrift

THE

DEVELOPMENT OF THRIFT

BY

MARY WILLCOX BROWN

GENERAL SECRETARY OF THE HENRY WATSON CHILDREN'S
AID SOCIETY OF BALTIMORE

New York

THE MACMILLAN COMPANY

LONDON: MACMILLAN & CO., Ltd.

1899

Norwood Press
J. S. Cushing & Co. — Berwick & Smith
Norwood Mass. U.S.A.

In Grateful Memory

OF

JOHN GLENN

PREFACE

In treating a subject as broad as is that of the development of thrift, it has not been possible in the compass of a small volume to do more than outline the general scope of the various agencies that have been organized to encourage and stimulate the practice of thrift.

It is hoped, however, that workers in charitable societies and social settlements who are trying to build up the character of the poor by teaching them how to be independent, and workingmen who are making an effort to organize associations and clubs by means of which to accumulate savings and to make safe investments, will find many helpful suggestions in the following pages.

For those who wish to make a thorough study of the subject of savings agencies, of workingmen's insurance, and of building and loan associations, this little book may serve as a stepping-stone.

BALTIMORE, January, 1899.

CONTENTS

CHAPTER I

ix

CHAPTER VII

CHAPTER VIII

CHAPTER IX

———

THE

DEVELOPMENT OF THRIFT

CHAPTER I

THE THRIFT HABIT

PHILANTHROPY that works to make a permanent effect must have as its primal object the giving of freedom. Its end must be to "lift up the manhood of the poor" by making them independent physically, mentally, morally. A mere assuagement of a man's lot may under many conditions be all that it is possible for charity to accomplish, but wherever charity has to deal with those that are sound in mind and body, its work must be directed toward making each free, free to make use of his opportunities, free to shape his life's course.

There never has been found, and there never will be found in a complex civilization

any one agency that will free the poor from
the destruction that is wrought in them by
their own poverty; but whichever of the various methods for their uplifting be chosen,
either by organizations or by individuals, those
only will be successful that are founded on
the belief that a man must be made to help
himself by exercising his inherent power and
by husbanding his own resources.

The laboring classes and many of their
friends have objected to the latter half of this
statement, *i.e.* that a man must help himself
by husbanding his resources, because the practice of thrift tends to lower wages, as well as,
by making the workingman a capitalist, to but-
tress the class he should supplant.   But on
the other hand, laborers in their unions have
developed thrift, on the ground that only by
saving from the wages of to-day for the demands of to-morrow can they make themselves independent of their employers, and
workingmen, individually, have freed themselves from dependence on others, because they
have schooled themselves to lay aside yearly
an increasing proportion of their monthly or

weekly earnings. Trades unions could never have effected what they have, unless they had been provided for the struggle with the ammunition furnished them from their own store of accumulated savings, and workingmen must learn, and have learned, to appreciate that what Benjamin Franklin said is true: that a workingman cannot become rich otherwise than by labor and saving, and that he that teaches to the contrary is a " poisoner."

A man who is on the margin of indebtedness or in debt cannot spend intelligently, for it is only when he has laid aside something that he can control his market, and, as Mr. Mackay says, by his thrifty expenditure both increase a demand for commodities, and increase and equalize the purchasing power of his community.

As this is no place to argue either for or against socialism, the objections that such men as Mr. Hyndman bring against the practice of thrift may not be considered, but it is hoped that in the following chapters it will be proved that the laboring classes are bettering their condition when they are enabled by larger opportunities to become in a manner their own capitalists.

A college settlement worker has said that ordinarily thrift is "rather demoralizing, because it is so absorbing, so limiting, so selfish." If she means by thrift a mere accumulation of money, one can but agree with her entirely, but fortunately thrift should not imply anything so sordid, and one does not have to subscribe to a theory that is "too narrow and too pessimistic for serious consideration."[1] Genuine thrift is not mere saving, but rather "postponed consumption," a laying aside not for the purpose of hoarding, but in order to make a future purchase. The small boy who pointed to a penny bank and said with intense pride, "I banks there," would have been no better for his emotion if his conception of what money is had not got beyond the belief that it is a commodity to hold. The value to him of his bank was that he was learning that money is more useful at one time than at another, and that by depositing it in some safe place, free

[1] Quoted from the letter of another college settlement resident.

from the allurements of the candy or the cigarette shop, he was reserving it for a more profitable use. The whole secret of right thrift lies in the formula: *Save wisely, so as to be able to spend judiciously in a time of need which will probably be greater than that of the present.*

Saving is not therefore, in itself, an economic virtue, but it is the "symbol and the instrument" of a man's independence, and "if the workman is to emerge from his present position and become a sharer in the gains of capital, he must in the first instance learn to save."[1] If he do not, he is enjoying the present at the expense of the future. A frugal man will exercise control, so as to put by something for the exigencies of the future, and by his self-denial he will gain the right to draw a self-earned livelihood when his working days are over. To forecast the needs of to-morrow, denying oneself to-day, so as to be prepared to meet the future demand, is no easy matter, and requires both knowledge and foresight, but he that has learned to discipline himself is the freedman.

[1] Professor J. E. Cairnes.

The poor are not naturally unthrifty, as Mr. Loch says, but lack opportunities. They are ignorant of how to use what they have, and their want of wisdom causes them to perish. They are placed in a wretched material environment, and their minds as well as their bodies become stunted; what they need is a wider outlook on life, and the opportunity to develop the best that is in them. But it is only by the well trained that the most can be made of the openings of life, and, therefore, the hope of the charity worker is centred in the child, who must be equipped for the struggle of life by a teaching that really fits him to grasp every chance that is given him to make his way and to hold his own. It is useless to preach thrift to one who has shouldered responsibilities he has not strength or fortitude to bear, but by being taught the value of practising wise economy and of exercising self-denial, the child may become father of the man that will not assume grave responsibilities until he feels that he can meet his obligations.

The unthriftiness of the well-to-do is proof

that thrift is not dependent on the size of a man's income, and as one of the great factors of education is example, the well-to-do, if they wish to promote provident habits in the poorer classes, must begin by being provident themselves.[1] It is encouraging to learn on good authority, that persons engaged in philanthropic work almost "inevitably become more simple and frugal in their own way of living," but in spite of this hopeful tendency, the poor have constantly before them the example of the wastefulness of the rich, who in their homes and out of them are showing how little care they take to be frugal in their own expenditures. The rich man does not feel the effect of his extravagance as does the poor man, because his purse yields him a margin for imprudent spending. He may not appreciate the results of his extravagance, but his example is contagious, and in the kitchen of the laborer is seen the effect of the wastefulness of the capitalist.

Few charity workers realize, when they urge

[1] Mr. George C. T. Bartley, "The Work of Charity in Promoting Provident Habits."

young girls to take up domestic service, how poor is the teaching in economy that a servant gets in the majority of homes that she enters. Though an effort is being made to improve domestic service, by making housekeepers wiser in their management, there is great work to be done before the homes of the rich will become good examples of economic living to the poor. In our charities, also, may be found the stamp of national extravagance. Apart from the excessive expenditures in many institutions and organizations, it must surely be demoralizing to many of the recipients of alms to read or to hear of the amount of money that has been spent in organizing a charity ball or bazaar. If the seeker for doles is taught that his patrons are able to spend so largely of their time and their money to net such a relatively small sum, no wonder he is willing to hold out his hand incessantly for more. He is merely getting his cue from the practices rather than from the preachings of his betters. Each one that wishes to teach the poor how to save, must learn that it should be said of him : —

"This noble ensample to his sheep he yaf,
  That first he wroghte and afterward he taughte."

The poor should be able to say that they are not asked to practise what the rich themselves have not tried to learn.

I suppose it is true for all times, in spite of the teachings of social reformers, that "every man is as lazy as he dares to be," and that unless the poor are taught to fear the consequences of their own improvidence they will not try to make provision for the future. Nothing can make people so improvident as the belief that there is very little to be gained by self-denial; indiscriminate giving of relief will always have the effect of lessening the number of the independent and of "encouraging the poor to keep untidy and dirty homes." The working classes are willing to provide for themselves if an unwise charity does not offer a bonus to incompetence. True charity should therefore be sagacious and by careful study of the conditions that surround any one who seems to be in need should get "hints for beneficence." An opportunity to acquire property, not merely to hold it as a gift, often teaches a man to make a valiant effort to become his own benefactor and to husband what he has had the pain of acquiring.

In the "Anatomy of a Tenement Street"[1] it is shown how the multiplication of charities is one of the causes of proverty. The street is a little city in itself, having its own history, which is quite distinct from that of the busy city that surges near it. The standard of living is low, the pleasures are such as do not really invigorate the dwellers; the squalor and the immorality tend to lower the vigor of the people; but though there is ample room for healthful reform, Charity can do nothing if she merely with skirts held high walk once a week through the street with note-book in her hand, and smoked glasses on her nose. Though she open her purse and scatter alms from her full basket, she will learn and teach nothing helpful unless she stop long enough to find out what is the life of these people, what are their daily hopes and fears, their genuine shortcomings, and their real human

[1] Alvan T. Sanborn, "Anatomy of a Tenement Street," Andover House Bulletin, No. 6.

qualities. Charity will be made to give all that she offers, and will receive nothing in return but a "tangled web of deceit," if she content herself with the superficial survey of the street. But the fatal mistake made by the charity that "means well" rather than "does well" is not that it learns to distrust human nature, but that by treating the poor as irresponsible members of society, it teaches them to be improvident, and to look for money as the reward of their thoughtlessness. Such indiscriminate relief "prevents the development of benefit insurance and savings agencies,"[1] and so holds the poor man down instead of lifting him up.

The lesson that each man must provide for himself is a hard one for the philanthropist to teach and for the poor man to learn. Nevertheless, even as in a primitive state each man must realize that his survival depends on his own energy and thrift, so in a civilized society each man must learn that he has to make his own way, though his civilized companions will and should be kinder to him

[1] H. Fawcett, "Pauperism: its Causes and Remedies."

than were the barbarous ones to his pro-
genitors.

The great incentive to him in his work will
be a clear knowledge of the benefits that are
to come to him from his labors, for "the sweat
of industry would dry and die but for the end
it works to." So soon as a little property is
acquired, that in itself will act as an incentive
to make further effort seem worth while, and
it will then constantly be found easier to lay
aside a little for the demands of that "unknown to-morrow." The practising of thrift
in one direction will be found to encourage
the practising of it in others, and saving will
be realized to be no hardship when it is learned
that present denial is going to make possible
some future gratification. On the other hand,
improvidence will be seen to work destruction,
and, whether through ignorance or wantonness,
thriftlessness will be seen to bring suffering
and disgrace. Ignorance! that is the key of
the difficulty that meets the charity worker who
is trying to teach frugality and providence. It
is very difficult, if not impossible, to inculcate
high ideals of life when there is no conception

of what life is, or to bring a man to realize
the sense of his manhood, when there is in
him no wish to be independent. Then, also,
when the daily wage is so small that it does
not meet the daily needs, and when lack of
work has brought with it accumulation of debts,
it seems impossible ever to hope to make earnings equal to expenditures, much less exceed
them. Besides, there is the large class of
workers that have to live on an intermittent
income, and, as Mrs. Bosanquet has said, "It
takes a very high order of intellect to be self-
supporting"[1] when the amount and regularity
of the wages cannot be foretold.

In the face of these great difficulties, wrought
by ignorance and lack of opportunity, the charity worker must strive to develop character by
increasing opportunities and by strengthening
purpose, and while realizing that in all classes
there is a residuum that has an "absence of
clear ideas, of looking before or after, of any
form of self-control or continuous application,"[2]
his constant effort must be to lessen the num-

[1] "Aspects of the Social Problem," p. 97.
[2] *Ibid.*, p. 111.

ber of the residuum in his small sphere of usefulness. He must try to make one individual, at least, see more clearly his present and his future needs, and aim by his own energy to provide for himself.

CHAPTER II

WHERE the difficulties of inculcating the habit of thrift are so great it is only by individual effort that one can hope to meet with success. The Charity Organization Society tries to train men and women to realize the needs of the poor and to carry to them, not as a body, but as individuals, the lesson the poor can learn from being brought into personal relations with such as have had larger opportunities and broader outlook on life than they. The visitor learns in order that he may teach, and though he meets the members of his "family" as man to man, his work as an individual is made more effective because he has back of him the energy and the enlightenment of an organization that does not lose sight of the fact that its own education is incomplete, and that it must continue to learn even while it is teaching the poor. The Charity Organization

Society realizes that to teach thrift the friendly visitor must go to each family separately and by careful study and by sympathetic insight must learn to know its needs and its capabilities.

The task of the visitor will not be a light one nor need she [1] expect to have any immediate influence. But gradually she may hope to effect a change for the better by enlarging the ideas and by developing the character of those with whom she is working.

As the first requisite is that the family be treated as a unit, it will not do for the visitor to call on the wife only, but she must manage to see the husband as well, so that she may be able to get a general idea of the physiognomy of the family. This is not the place to show what is the general field of work for the friendly visitor, for that subject is thoroughly treated in the other volume in this series,[2] but, from the standpoint of the thrift teacher, she must realize that it will not do to urge the mem-

[1] It is to be regretted that the number of the women so largely exceeds that of the men visitors as to make it sound rather absurd to continue to use the masculine gender, even as the English equivalent of the common gender.

[2] Mary E. Richmond, "Friendly Visiting among the Poor."

bers of her family to save until she has carefully considered whether there is a surplus that can be safely withdrawn from the sum that goes to meet the daily needs. There are thrifty housewives who will feed themselves and their children on bread alone, so that the father may keep up his club dues or the insurance agent collect his weekly premiums. Here the visitor must show that it is not a wise economy which tends to lower the vitality of any member of the family, in order that provision may be made for the future.

In urging saving on the family, the visitor must be careful not in her zeal to speak as if the mere act of saving were in itself creative of anything. "A penny saved is a penny earned" is not a fair statement, because a cent that is laid aside does not add anything to the income, unless it be saved from an unproductive use in order that it may be well spent. Mere putting money in bank should not be looked on as an end in itself, and the visitor must be cautious to avoid the fallacy of teaching that the act of saving is anything more than a means.

c

A Charity Organization Society worker in London would feel that a family is in a very bad way if its head were not insured in some friendly society. It is to be hoped that in this country such beneficent agencies may be encouraged to enlarge their usefulness and that the friendly visitor may consider it to be part of her mission to use good fraternal societies as one of the mediums for the receipt of the savings of her family.

One of the chief missions of the visitor is to find employment for the man. After this is done, her work must lie principally with the wife, and her usefulness to the family will largely lie in her power of showing the housekeeper how wisely to spend the husband's wages.

What she must carefully avoid, however, is any "grandmotherly interference" in the expenditure of the income. If she urge the wife to join fuel or flour clubs, she must consider whether the independence of the family will be assailed by the members being taught to look to charity to supplement the earnings. The two great items of expenditure will be found to be rent and food, lesser items, fuel and clothing, and whether there is to be any surplus for saving and for pleasure will depend largely on the good management of the housewife.

Economists agree that "twenty per cent of the earnings of the head of the family ought to be the maximum expenditure for rent in cities,"[1] but many workingmen are spending a larger proportion of their income for rent, and are getting a very poor return for their money. The friendly visitor may be able to prove that it is an economy to live in a healthy locality, and that it is sometimes cheaper to move to the suburbs than to stay in the centre of the city. It is difficult to get people to change their neighborhood, but the advantage of house-owning is sometimes a powerful inducement, so that a man who is getting on his feet may be readily induced to buy his own house through a coöperative building association, and by so doing be able to move into a more desirable part of his town.

[1] Eighth Special Report of the Commissioner of Labor, "The Housing of the Working People," p. 422.

The prejudices of the poor make it often very difficult for the visitor to get the housewife to introduce any change in the buying or the preparing of food. Physical conditions have, however, so much to do with the thriftiness or unthriftiness of the poor, and increased opportunities for better living, which are furnished by healthy homes and by wholesome food, have so great an influence not only on the earning capacity but on the saving power of the man, that the visitor should not allow herself to be easily discouraged. What the housewife needs is to be shown how to spend her income, and the visitor must patiently undertake the task.

As "the large majority of families in this country are said to have not over $500 a year to live upon,"[1] how important it is that if possible not more but less than half the income should be expended on food, and that whatever is spent should go to provide a nutritious diet.

The appended table shows what proportion

[1] W. O. Atwater, "Foods : Nutritive Value and Cost," Farmer's Bulletin, No. 23, U. S. Department of Agriculture, p. 20.

of a workingman's income is expended on subsistence in such a state as Massachusetts: —

MASSACHUSETTS[1]

Annual income	Amount expended for food	Per cent expended for food
$350 to $400	$224 to $256	64
450 to 600	284 to 378	63
600 to 750	360 to 450	60
750 to 1200	420 to 672	56
above 1200	672	51

. The cheapest food is not, of course, that
which actually cost the least money, but that
which yields the most nutriment for the least
outlay. The visitor, therefore, should understand what is a dietary that will supply a
wholesome amount of nutriment, before she
tries to show the housewife how to regulate
the expenses of her table.

The Orange Bureau of Associated Charities
has published a leaflet for the use of its visitors, who appreciate that the poor are in need
of instruction as to how to spend their in-

[1] *Ibid.* The amount of a workingman's income which shall
be expended on food varies with the locality and with other
conditions.

comes. The possible living expenses of a family of six persons — man, wife, and four children between the ages of eight and one — are calculated on the basis of an annual income of $312, or $6 a week.

Rent, $5.00 a month	$60.00
Fuel and light	16.30
Food	171.97
Clothes and incidentals	63.73
	$312.00

A visitor would have to work very patiently and diligently before she could make the members of her family so painstaking that each cent could be accurately accounted for; but if such authorities as Mr. Edward Atkinson and Mr. Carroll D. Wright repeatedly call attention to the fact that the proportion of income that the poor expend on food is much too large, the visitor should try to teach her family how to be wisely frugal in this direction.

Attention is frequently called to the economy of French housewives, and the statement is made that the waste in an American kitchen would supply food enough for a French family. This has been said to be exaggerated, but whether it is or not, it points two morals : first, that any good housekeeper should have pride in making the statement false in her own case, and secondly, that in growing more frugal she must guard against harmful economy. Mr. Brassey, the English contractor, in his well-known experiment with the French navvies, found that the working capacity of the English laborer to that of the French was as five to three, and the greater earning power of the former was largely a question of more sustaining food. The question of food then is a question of knowledge, and the problem is how to teach the poor the "elementary facts regarding food and nutrition."

Taste in dress is hardly a subject to be treated under thrift, but the visitor can teach in this direction that a stitch in time saves nine, which though trite is true, and that a discarded garment may sometimes be utilized to make a gown for a younger child or to serve as material for patching.

Three insidious foes of the poor are said to be: the instalment plan, chattel mortgages, and credit. In the following chapters it will be seen that the first is often a method of purchase that is not only feasible but economical, and that many a man has been able to buy a house on the instalment plan, which he could not have otherwise procured. There is, however, both a wise and an unwise use of this method of purchasing, and much money is wasted by the poor in buying useless articles thrust on them by persistent pedlers and shopkeepers, who try to cheat them into a belief that a payment of ten or twenty-five cents a week can make no impression on the weekly salary, and that some knickknack or a valuable piece of furniture is being got for almost nothing. By such fallacious arguments they are led to make purchases for which they are not able to pay. A visitor can be of great help, if she show how very dearly such purchases are made, and how the interest on the deferred payments adds to the real cost of the article. The chief danger of buying on the instalment plan lies in the fact that the poor are as a rule very hopeful of the future, and feel, therefore, that something will be sure to turn up to make it easy for the new obliga-

tion to be met. The same may be said of
money borrowed on a chattel mortgage. A
poor man is often benefited by negotiating a
loan, when the money is borrowed to meet
a temporary difficulty or to be put to some
productive use, but here again the visitor must
show what is the actual cost of the loan, and,
if possible, she must protect him whom she is
trying to help against the extortionate charge of
a usurious money-lender. If the money is to be
borrowed, she should try to bring the workingman into communication with some agency
that will lend money at a reasonable rate, and if
the money has been borrowed from some company that charges an exorbitant rate of interest,
she should secure legal aid before trying to
make an equitable settlement of the loan.

An Englishman has calculated that the
amount of money spent by a workingman
in supporting himself for a day and a half
would keep him two days if he were to buy
for cash instead of on credit, and for three
days if he were to buy in large instead of in
small quantities. Coal and groceries bought
in large quantities will be found to be much

more economical, unless the housewife be tempted by a full bin and larder to be lavish in her use of them, and the doing away with the credit book will mean not only cheaper but more judicious purchasing. When the poor are forced, because of the tyranny of the credit system, to buy at some one store, they are not only denied the privilege of choosing what they prefer, but are often forced to accept adulterated articles of food. A woman who, for years, had been at the mercy of the corner grocery-man, to whom she always owed a large bill, told me that when, some months ago, she moved into the suburb of the city in which she lived, she determined to buy in the future only for cash. She said, "It's much cheaper, because you do without all sorts of little things, and you don't get anything unless you've got the money to pay." She is slowly paying her back bill at the grocer's, and is trying to induce a married sister to close her credit account at "the store." She firmly believes that the cash system is the cheaper and the better.

It has been suggested that American housewives should keep a careful account of their expenditures. Perhaps some visitor may be able to induce her family to make entries in a day-book,[1] which can be carefully arranged by her. Into this book should be entered the amount of the family income, and the daily expenditures for food and fuel, and the monthly or the weekly outlay for rent and clothes, as well as the surplus laid aside for a savings account or for recreation. Such a diary, if faithfully kept, would be of great use, not only to the housewife herself, in showing her how to regulate her expenses, but to the visitor in teaching her to meet the needs of other families she may visit.

When the visitor becomes discouraged and even disheartened by the difficulties that she meets with in her dealings with the father and mother, she may hope for better success with the children. She may urge them to put aside a few pennies, so that

[1] C. R. Henderson, "The Social Spirit in America," appendix.

American Journal of. Sociology, March, 1897, p. 662.

they may acquire a habit of saving and have some small accumulated sum to draw on when a pair of shoes is needed or some prized tool or other useful article. Such purchases will relieve the family purse, or add to the usefulness of the child. By teaching the children to save, two important results may be attained, — the parents, influenced by the example of the children, may be taught to lay aside, and the children themselves, even as they save the small pennies from some harmful or useless expenditure, may be learning self-denial, which will make them better and more useful men and women than their forebears. The habit of counting the cost will tend to prevent imprudent marriages, and will add to the number of those who will be able throughout life to remain independent.

As with the grown people, so, also, with the children, the visitor will have carefully to study their real interests, and she will have to guard against letting a disposition to save deprive them of any advantages, hygienic or educational, or force them prematurely to enter the labor market. The latter danger is very real, and the visitor will have to watch her own inclinations, so as never to let the exigencies of the present urge her to make the children wage-earners before they have got sufficient physical strength or mental training to' make them fit to begin their working life. Perhaps, through the children the visitor may be able to teach her family to appreciate the three *p*'s, — paint, pictures, plants. The educational effect of clean paint, of some bright pictures on the walls, and of some hardy plants in a sunny window will be seen in the increased thriftiness of the family. A woman once said that she could reform the farmers, if she were permitted to go from one farm-house to another with a paint-pot; and another says that wonders may be wrought by giving a child a bucket of whitewash and showing him where to apply it. Many persons would agree in part with the former, and wholly with the latter, if they had watched the effect wrought in town and country by a little new paint, or whitewash,

a few flowers, and some gay bits of decora-
tion..

Four simple rules might be given by the visitor to her family: "Spend less than you earn,
pay ready money, never anticipate uncertain
profits, keep regular accounts." In many
cases, it would be a farce for the visitor to urge
the observance of the first rule, but when the
income is variable she may say: "In a season
of plenty save for the season of want." A
great many laborers make a good income at
some one season of the year, but, through lack
of foresight or self-denial, the ready money is
quickly spent, and a time follows when charity
is called on to intervene so that the family need
not be forced to suffer the effects of its own
carelessness. The visitor should strive to prevent the waste by showing the necessity of
each man's bearing the responsibilities he has
assumed.

The task of the visitor in teaching thrift is
no easy one. She will meet with failure and
bitter disappointment, and will often seem to
touch success only to find that "wishers and
woulders are no good householders," for char-

acter has to be developed before a promise has the power to bind. But she will be rewarded if she teach some one family to be self-respecting, and make the members realize their obligations and strive to provide for the demands not only of the present, but of the future.

CHAPTER III

INDIVIDUALISTIC SAVINGS AGENCIES

A FRENCH sociologist has carefully elaborated the theory that the social growth of man has its root in economic life, and that, therefore, the first social phenomena to be developed were the economic, and that only gradually have been added, in the order named, the genetic, the artistic, the religious, the moral, the juridic, and the political. If such a theory be accepted, one has to appreciate that it is very difficult to effect a change in habits which are regulated by economic traditions, and that conversely it is in material prosperity that men's interests are really centred. Let it be clearly realized, therefore, that if one wish to change the conditions that surround the poor, one must not attempt to overturn suddenly their economic life, and that one must have a very definite knowledge of the conditions that influence the class among whom one feels called on to work. The worker in order to be successful must appeal, in a rational way, to the most vital interests of the poorer classes, and he must look only for a gradual raising of the standard of life. Though an appeal to the pocket may seem to be a low basis for action, let the philanthropist appreciate that the surest way to reach any class of persons is to make it realize that by following a prescribed course there will be a financial gain.

Reformers who have appreciated that men must be reached through the natural interests before they can assimilate mental and moral teaching, have tried to develop savings agencies, not only that the savers may have a reserve fund for future contingencies, but that they may have the consciousness of being removed by their savings from the burden of relief-receiving. Just as far as the savings agencies are divorced from mere relief-giving societies and from all so-called charities that offer a bonus to improvidence and thriftlessness will they develop not only economy, but also the higher forces of life. The nearer savings asso-

D

ciations come to making the poor agents in "bettering their own condition" the more nearly will they reach the ideal toward which the most clear sighted of their promoters have been working.

Savings agencies may be divided broadly into two classes, — individualistic and mutual. By repeating what has just been said, that the poor must be taught to be their own agents in bettering their condition, it will be appreciated that coöperation in its right sense is the higher form of philanthropic work. Individualistic savings agencies reach each depositor separately, and do not make the poor man a part, except to a small degree, of the society from which he is to draw his principal and interest. Though this form of saving is not as educational as the mutual, it is its necessary forerunner, and prepares the way for the more advanced stage.

Individualistic savings funds may be divided into four classes: *a*. Savings banks; *b*. Postal savings and stamp savings banks; *c*. Collecting savings banks; *d*. Savings funds for the wholesale buying of fuel, flour, etc.

Savings Banks.   Since 1816, when the first savings bank, the Boston Provident Savings Institution, was established in the United States, the growth of savings banks has been almost continuous.   In only two years since 1820 has there been any retrogression in the movement; namely, in 1878 and in 1894. During the former year the decrease in the number of depositors was 132,078, and in the latter, 52,912.   The founding of such banks has been the result of a belief that the poor need a place of deposit for their savings and that the result of having no depositary is to make them reckless in the expenditure of their earnings.   As early as 1803 Mr. Malthus in his essay on " Population " drew attention to this fact, and somewhat later in the century another Englishman claimed that " contemporary with the growth of savings banks, we have seen a growth of civilization among the poorer classes."

In 1820 there were [1] 10 savings banks in the

---

[1] The following figures are taken from the Annual Report of the Comptroller of the Currency, 1897, Vol. I., pp. xxv, xxvi, 566, 567, 568.

United States having deposits amounting to $1,138,576, which had been intrusted to them by 8635 savers. In 1897 reports were received by the Comptroller of the Currency from 980 savings banks, 668 of which are mutual institutions, 312 stock savings banks. The aggregate resources of these banks are $2,198,824,474. The total deposits are $1,939,376,035, — the number of depositors, 5,201,132. The average amount credited to a depositor was, in 1820, $131.86, and is at present, $372.88.

These banks are distributed as follows : —

MUTUAL SAVINGS BANKS.		STOCK SAVINGS BANKS	
New England States	457	District of Columbia .	1
Eastern States .	. 200	Southern States .	. 34
Southern States .	. 1	Western States .	. 212
Western States .	. 10	Pacific States . .	. 65
	668		312

In New York about twenty-five per cent of the population deposit in savings banks, or 1,736,968 persons, and in Massachusetts about fifty per cent, or 1,340,668.

In the seven Southern States into which savings banks have been carried, 68,871 per-

sons have placed in the thirty-five banks mentioned $10,479,080.

"The principle upon which *savings banks* are
founded interferes with no individual action,
saps no individual self-reliance. It prolongs
childhood by no proffered leading-string. . . .
It does not attempt to foster the infant habit
of saving by the unnatural addition of a penny
to every penny laid by."[1]   This is as true now
as it was fifty years ago, but the successors
of the early promoters of savings banks have
had to learn that the holders of small incomes
cannot be always trusted to make use of the
safe place of deposit that is provided for them.
A bank needs oftentimes to be brought to the
very door of the small saver; for even if he
has a desire to save a part of his income,
the habit of accumulating savings in a non-
interest-bearing jug or stocking will not be
overcome unless he is able easily to make use
of a more reliable place of deposit.

To those that are on the margin of thriftlessness, the savings bank has to go as a persistent reminder of the necessity that lies on

[1] W. R. Greg, *Edinburgh Review*, 1853, p. 406.

every man to provide for his own future needs.
It was the realization of this fact that made
the English government establish the Post-
Office Savings Banks, and induced some public-
spirited men in Baltimore to open a Provident
Savings Bank, which would be at the very
doors of the poor and would be a sure teacher
of economy and a tireless promoter of thrift.

The Post-Office Savings Banks of England
were established by act of Parliament in 1861.
Mr. Whitbread, a member of the House of
Commons, introduced a bill into Parliament as
early as 1807, "for establishing a Fund and
Assurance Office for Investing the Savings of
the Poor," but it was only after fifty years of
agitation that the government undertook to
receive the small deposits of the English
people.

Two great advantages of the system are:
that the investor may feel that his deposit is
absolutely safe, and that he can find an office
of the bank in any part of the kingdom. He
can deposit at any one of the 11,867 offices,
and in order to withdraw his money is not
obliged to go to the office in which it was

deposited. The system is an endless chain, and the depositors may make connection with the chain at any one of its links.

One of the objections that has been made to the system is that it is very complicated, but the formalities that have to be met in either depositing or withdrawing money are not considerable enough to act as a barrier· to the success of the system, which is proved by the fact that one person out of seven in England has money deposited in the post-office savings bank; and any one wishing to deposit any sum from a shilling upwards, may do so by applying at the nearest post-office between the hours of 8 a.m. and 8 p.m. As much as £50 may be deposited in any one year, and each depositor may have at any one time, £200, including interest, to his credit. When this limit has been exceeded, the balance is invested in government stock, unless the depositor directs that other use be made of his money. The interest on the money is two and a half per cent per annum. For the convenience of the small savers, penny stamps are issued by the post-office, and these are redeemed when a shilling's worth of stamps has been bought.

Withdrawals may be made in person or by order.[1] The local office furnishes withdrawal forms for the use of the depositors, and these are sent free of cost to the chief office in London. Should there be immediate need of the money, the depositor may make withdrawal by telegraph, though he has to bear the expense of the message. If the sum called for does not exceed £10, it may be got on the same day that the telegram is sent; if it exceeds this amount, it will be received on the day following. Children over seven years of age may deposit and withdraw money in their own names; under seven years of age, the deposits must be made by guardians. Not only may individuals deposit, but also societies and penny banks to an unlimited amount.

The post-office savings banks collect divi-

[1] The National Penny Bank, London, also offers to any person living in any part of England, Wales, Scotland, or Ireland the privilege of opening an account at the head office in London and of depositing and withdrawing money by post. The depositor when sending his book has to enclose postage stamps for its return.

dends for those that have invested through their agency in government stock, and also make sale of the stock, charging for the latter' service a small commission.   Very little use is made, however, of this right "to accumulate £500 in consols in addition to the £200, which may be accumulated in deposits," the reason given being that the class that uses the post-office savings banks does not care to invest in securities that vary in price.

These banks offer every facility to him who wishes to save, and their effect is far-reaching; but in the evident fact that a general use of the banks enormously increases the amounts held by them, lies a danger that is being real-ized.   Annually many thousands of pounds are added to the people's money held by the post-office savings banks, — an amount that now reaches £108,098,641 [1]; and this vast sum, which is invested in consols, is withdrawn from the capital that is held by the people directly for their own use.   It is also neces-sary to call attention to the statement that

[1] Amount due to depositors on 31st of December, 1896, Forty-third Report of the Postmaster-General.

the "post-office savings bank is really a charity." The nation pays the two and one-half per cent that is needed to meet the expenses of management.[1] This expense was formerly met by the difference between "the deposit interest and the interest which the nation could get for its money"; but as the interest on consols is now low, and their price high, no sufficient margin is left to meet current expenses. Such a condition is not inherent in the system. Italy, for instance, makes a profit from her post-office savings banks, after paying five per cent interest on consols; but the fact that England does lose by her savings banks should be carefully considered by our government, if it should undertake the savings-bank business.

Since the inauguration of the system in England, it has been adopted by all of the British

[1] "Notwithstanding *the* reduction of the rate of working expenses, the rise in the price of consols has caused some embarrassment, and the whole business, after payment of expenses and 2½ % interest to depositors, has shown a deficit of £3791, which has been voted by Parliament. This is the first year since the establishment of the Savings Bank that any deficit has occurred." Forty-third Report of the Postmaster-General, p. 14. This last assertion has been challenged by the *London Times* and by careful students of financial problems.

colonies and by all of the leading countries, except Germany,[1] Switzerland, and the United States. Repeated efforts have been made by postmaster-generals, by senators, by representatives in Congress, by state officials, and by various charitable societies to introduce the system into the United States. Its adoption was first proposed by Postmaster-General Creswell, in 1871, and two years later a bill was introduced into the House of Representatives by Mr. Horace Maynard of Tennessee, asking for the establishment and the maintenance of a "National Savings Depository as a Branch of the Post-Office Department." Since then, sixteen different bills have been introduced into the United States Congress asking for the establishment of the system. Postmaster-General Gary strongly urged the adoption of the postal savings depository, so that the question of the expediency of the government's becoming the receiver of the small savings of the nation has recently been before the public.

The need of increasing the number of sav-

[1] Germany has many municipal savings banks.

ings banks has been seen, but it can be questioned whether it be wise for the federal government to undertake any more business enterprises. The promoters of the system will do well to bear in mind that the absorption by the government of business enterprises leads to state socialism, and also that, according to the last annual report of the Post-master-General, the deficit in the Post-office Department was $11,411,779.65.[1] Let it further be realized that the establishment of such banks will not be a relief in the parts of the country where currency is scarce.

The *Stamp Savings Societies* in this country may be classed as philanthropic, commercial, and philanthropic-commercial. To the first class belongs the Penny Provident Fund of New York City; to the second, such enterprises as were organized in the West by the Citizens' Savings Bank of Detroit; and to the third, the Provident Savings Bank of Baltimore. There are many modifications of these

[1] Report of the Postmaster-General, July 1, 1897. Report for the year ending June 30, 1898, will not be issued until December, 1898.

several plans, but they will serve to illustrate the workings of the Stamp Savings System in the United States.

The *Penny Provident Fund* was inaugurated because of the need that was felt by the friendly visitors of the New York Charity Organization Society of having some safe place of deposit for the small sums of money that were intrusted to them by the families visited. Only one of the New York savings banks would receive a deposit of less than one dollar, and it was realized that a new agency must be supplied to meet the needs of the poorer classes.

It is stated in a prospectus of the Fund that "The larger portion of the want and suffering *in all communities* is the direct result of a waste of small sums in unnecessary expenditures, and the failure to provide by laying up such sums, against the possible loss of work, or against accident or illness." It was designed, therefore, that these small sums should be got hold of, and that the depositors should be encouraged to open accounts in a savings bank.

The fund was established in 1889, and at present there are 321 stations circulating the stamps among 57,189 depositors. The fund operates not only in New York City, but in many other cities and towns, so that in South Carolina and Virginia, in Kentucky, Illinois, Colorado, and Iowa, and even in Canada, may be found branches of its work. In New York itself, stations are established in savings banks, churches, boys' and girls' clubs, friendly societies, college and university settlements, library associations, day nurseries, retail stores, charity organization society offices, and, most important of all, in many of the public and charitable schools. There is no difficulty attached to the opening of a station in either a rural or an urban community, for one of the chief merits of the system is that it entails no bookkeeping. Any one wishing to open a station may get the necessary supplies from the cashier.[1] Stamp cards, signature slips, rules for stamp stations, envelopes for cards and pass-books, circulars of information, may

[1] Miss Marian Messemer, 22d Street and Fourth Avenue, New York.

all be obtained free of charge, the only expense being that of transportation. The necessary outlay is for the stamps,[1] and these are paid for at their face value. After a supply of stamps is once bought, there need be no further outlay, unless the stock in hand is enlarged, for the deposits quickly make good the deficit.

No station is allowed to sell detached stamps lest they should be used for barter, and for the same reason cards and books are not transferable. As soon as a would-be depositor of one cent or more has signed the signature slip, he receives a stamped card on which are printed the rules and conditions that regulate his connection with the Fund. These rules advise him that money can be withdrawn only on presentation and surrender of the card at the stamp station where the deposit was made, that one week's notice may be required before money can be withdrawn, that no sum can be withdrawn less than the whole amount represented by the stamps attached to the card, and that no payment will be made if the card be lost or destroyed.

[1] Teachers may buy stamps on credit.

No interest is given on accounts, because
the object of the Fund is to encourage its depositors, as soon as each has accumulated $10,
to transfer his account to the regular savings
banks. The interest on the money invested
by the Fund is used to meet current expenses,
which annually exceed the receipts.

The collectors for the Fund are agents that
are ever on the alert to bring to the savings
bank the gradually accumulated pennies of
those that without such an agency would never
know that it was possible for them to hold a
bank account, but would feel, on the contrary,
that it was absurd for any one to assert that,
"Every one may have a bank account to draw
upon in time of need."

In 1897 the amount deposited was $74,253.98,
withdrawn, $69,323.94. The net deposit was
$36,235.48, the average account, about 63
cents.

The *Commercial Stamps Savings Banks* were
organized by the regular savings banks because
their promoters believed that the cost of equipment would be more than repaid by the credit
that would accrue to the banks from increasing

the number of depositors. They hoped that by encouraging young people to save, a future clientage would be provided that would bring great profit to the banks. Forbes, Thomas & Co., stamp equipment manufacturers, published circular letters to advertise the system, their letters being addressed to employers of labor, to teachers and to their pupils, to retail tradesmen, to wage earners, and to mothers of families. The gist of each appeal was that the person making use of the stamp savings system would receive some peculiar benefit from so doing. The system did not, however, prove a practical success, and four years ago the enterprise was abandoned, and out of 311 banks equipped, not one is known to be continuing the use of the system.[1]

The first bank to introduce the system was the Citizens' Savings Bank of Detroit, which in 1890 began the sale of stamps, and, as a result, in one year increased the number of its savings accounts from 720 to 5000. Though the bank intended to limit its workings to

[1] Report of William A. Forbes & Co., successors to Forbes, Thomas & Co., Detroit.

E

Detroit, such a demand came to it from merchants in other cities that it opened agencies in various places throughout Michigan. For a time the system was very popular, but in 1893, owing to the financial panic, the bank discontinued the sale of stamps, the demand for them having greatly decreased, and it has not since resumed this branch of work. The cashier of the bank writes: "It is possible that we may take it up again in prosperous times. We discontinued it because the cost of administration requires a certain volume of business in order to make it profitable. It was only the panic that interfered with the steady increase in the volume of this business."

The failure of the Citizens' Savings Bank, as well as of many other Western banks, to continue the sale of stamps in a time of financial stress, shows how inadequate a purely commercial system is to meet the needs of the very small savers. A bank that studies its own interest rather than that of its depositors will sacrifice the welfare of the latter whenever it realizes that the cost of administration is greater than the returns made to it by them.

The *Provident Savings Bank* of Baltimore, the first stamp savings bank established in the United States, was incorporated in 1886. Its threefold object is: to take the bank to the people; to make its hours convenient for them; and to receive small sums. As a bank, it is safe, convenient, profitable. It is in itself "a powerful promoter of thrift, and a constant enemy of extravagance and improvidence."

The deposits are made in a way very similar to that described in the case of the Penny Provident Fund, and the same rules and conditions have to be subscribed to. A child may deposit in his own name, subject to his own withdrawal, or his deposit may be made in the name of some guardian. No sum less than three dollars of the principal may be withdrawn unless it be to close an account, and no interest is granted on sums amounting to less than five dollars, or more than three thousand dollars. The bank has no stockholders, and is conducted solely in the interest of the depositors, the profits arising from the regular savings department being used to support the stamp savings system. The bank not only has branch offices in different parts of the city, but has forced its way into churches and clubs, Christian associations and charitable agencies, — in fact, wherever there is felt to be a need for the promotion of thrift by offering an easy means of saving. What distinguishes the working of the Penny Provident Fund and the Provident Savings Bank from other dime savings banks, is their aggressiveness. They work their way into places where money is scarce, and hunt diligently until they find the mites that in their keeping accumulate until they make an imposing total. The advantages of establishing a bank on a philanthropic-commercial basis are manifest, for the philanthropic impulse will assure the guarding of the interests of the depositors, and the commercial regulations will make the bank not only self-supporting but educational.

One of the stamp savings banks has printed on its stamp cards such mottoes as: "See what the dictionary says about 'provident,'" "Pennies make dollars," "A penny saved is a penny gained." It is doubtful whether such axioms have any educational value, but it is unfortunate that on the reverse side of the card should be printed in connection with other inducements to save: "Save for the flour club, save for the coal club." The fundamental object of a savings society, to make the users of it independent, can hardly be realized if the depositors in it are encouraged to withdraw their money in order to invest it in a society that is conducted on a purely philanthropic basis. No matter how well managed the flour or coal club may be, it can but be a stepping-stone to higher forms of saving, and a step backward in economic life is made, when the depositor withdraws his savings to use such an agency as a medium for procuring for himself one of the necessities of life at less than the market rate. "The flaccid dependence of the coddled poor" can never be transformed into rigid independence unless the promoters of various kinds of charity read into their methods the simple rules of business life.

Another error that has been made by a branch bank, one that is established in a boys' club, is to compute the interest on deposits, not according to the amount of the deposits, but according to their number. This is done so as to encourage the boys to deposit often, as is also the permission given to friends of the club to add to the savings bank interest by gifts of money or other prizes. It is to be hoped that some one of the boys may have enough independence to refuse the gift as did a sturdy Englishman who, on being told by a savings bank collector that his rector, the treasurer of the bank, had added to the amount of his interest, so as to encourage him to save, would accept only the business rate of interest. The granting of a bonus destroys the intrinsic benefit of the act of saving, and is besides a useless expenditure of money, for it has been proved that those who save in small amounts do not need the inducement of interest. The money accumulates too slowly for the interest to be looked on as an important addition to the bank balance.

As has been said, the time to ingraft thrift habits is when children are still young enough to be receptive of new teachings, and when they have not to unlearn thriftless habits. The intent to save has ordinarily to be acquired, and the child who is taught that he must deny himself a present gratification in order to meet a future need, has learned a lesson in economics which will serve him as a valuable implement with which to cut for himself a road to success in later years. The most important development of the stamp savings system is, therefore, its adoption as a part of the public school work. The movement to introduce the system has not as yet been very widespread, but great good has been accomplished wherever the teachers have taken the trouble to inaugurate the system and to carry it on. The Penny Provident Fund of New York has stations in eighteen public schools in New York City, and in public schools in New Rochelle and Plattsburg, New York, in Lakewood, New Jersey, in Greenwich and South Manchester, Connecticut, and in Evanston, Illinois. A very successful work in the public schools is being carried on in Lynn, Massachusetts, where the system was introduced as the result of the work of one woman. She presented the subject to the school board and got permission to have the teachers collect the children's savings. On certain days in each week the teachers sell the stamps before school opens or at recess. The principal of a school receives from the bank a quantity of stamps on credit, — say $50 worth, — and as he sells the stamps he gets a fresh supply, paying for them with the money received for the last consignment. It is only at the end of the school year that a final settlement is made with the bank. The sole expense of the system is the printing of cards and stamps, and the pay of a bank clerk for one hour each day during the school year, and for an hour and a half a week during the vacation. The clerk's salary is between $150 and $200 a year, and he is given desk room in the office of the Lynn Charity Organization Society.

In Grand Rapids, Michigan, where the system has been introduced into thirty-two public schools, it is so simply conducted that not more than ten minutes is required by a teacher to complete the business at each weekly depositing. Each child has his folder in which he sticks the stamp that is given him as a receipt for the money handed by him to the teacher. After the sale, the money is put into a coin bag and is sent to the principal to be delivered by him to the bank messenger, who calls at each school for the deposits and returns to the principal an equivalent in stamps for the money received. The folders, coin bags, and stamps are furnished by the bank.

Such a plan is so simple that it does not entail much labor on any teacher, though it necessarily gives extra work to a class of men and women on whose time great demand is made. It is, therefore, only when moved by a feeling of keen interest in the individual welfare of the pupils, and when the teacher realizes that his responsibility is not connected solely with the mental development of his charges, that he will be willing to undertake such a work. To the teacher that has been annoyed by the pupils' persistently buying cheap candy and cigarettes, it must be a great relief to see the pennies put into a savings bank. The opening of a savings bank account in a school has a direct effect on the sales of the small candy shops in its neighborhood, and the owners of such shops are said to be the only enemies of the system.

The first school savings bank was established in 1834 in France, — a country where it has long been realized, as Albert Shaw says, that "the multiplication of savings banks . . . is a factor of prime importance in the conservation of the national wealth." In 1875, the system was introduced into the elementary schools of Paris, and at present the Epargne Scolaire collects 150,000 francs a year. The school savings banks have been very successful in Belgium, from which country they have spread to other continental countries. In England after the education department issued circular letters calling the attention of the teachers to the importance of the school savings banks, their number increased during a year from 2629 to 6383. There, as elsewhere, these banks have proved to be valuable auxiliaries of the post-office savings banks, and the teachers have cordially coöperated with the school board and with the post-office savings banks in developing

the system.   In Manchester,[1] Birmingham, and
Liverpool the school banks have been peculiarly successful.

In 1885, Mr. J. H. Thiry of Long Island
City introduced the system of school savings
banks into one of the public schools of Long
Island City.   Within a year, his system, which
was established after a careful study of the
French, Belgian, German, English, and Italian
systems, was in use in all the schools of
the city.   In his thirteenth annual report, Mr.
Thiry states that his system is now in practice
in seventy-six cities and villages in New York
State, in Massachusetts, in Connecticut, in
Pennsylvania, in New Jersey, in North Dakota,
in Michigan, and in the state of Washing-
ton, and that since 1885 $530,319.58 has
been deposited, $350,668.56 withdrawn, the
balance in bank in March, 1898, being $179,-
651.02.

Mr. Thiry believes that the success of the
system is dependent on the efficiency of the

---

[1] For an interesting account of the Manchester School Savings Banks, see Report International Congress of Charities,
Sec. 6, "The Organization of Charities," p. 384.

school board, on the zeal and untiring interest of the teachers, and on the coöperation of the savings banks. The object of the management should not be the accumulation of savings, but rather the educating of the child in habits of thrift and self-denial. It should be made, therefore, an integral part of the school work, and should be undertaken always by the teacher and never by the bank collector. For the same reason the collections should be made during school hours, preferably at the opening of school on Monday morning, and the teacher should frequently point out the economic effect of the regular saving, and should make use of the opportunity offered, by instilling into the pupils the desire to become independent. If the teacher try to impress these broad principles on the children, there will be no danger of a spirit of miserliness being fostered.

Some of the results of the introduction of the system are: more cheerful attendance of the pupils and less tardiness on Monday mornings; a better understanding between teachers and parents; an increase in the salaries of the teachers (when the school board has appreciated the value of the ethical work done by them); and a realization on the part of the pupils of the value of self-restraint and of money.

Miss Agnes Lambert, the English authority on school savings banks, gives three cardinal rules for the use of the promoters of the system. "(1) The utmost simplicity and safety of machinery; (2) the minimum of labor and responsibility for teachers; (3) an educational exercise." [1]   Miss Lambert, M. de Malarce, the French promoter of school savings banks, Pastor Senckel, the German "Apostle" of the system, and Mr. Thiry in this country, advocate the abolition of the stamp system of collecting, as they severally feel that the direct system of deposit is more businesslike, and therefore more educational. One more point should be mentioned, that only the children's savings be received, and that the pupils be encouraged to deposit only what represents their own accumulations. Before the system is introduced into a school, circulars should be sent to the

[1] Agnes Lambert, "School Bank Manual," p. 7.

parents of the pupils, in which the system, and its object, is fully explained.[1]

At the risk of being tedious it must be repeated that the success of the stamp saving system is dependent on the vigilance and energy of its directors, and that unless constant efforts be made to stimulate thrift, the undertaking will be abortive, as has been shown in the case of the Citizens' Savings Bank of Detroit. It must, also, be appreciated that the opening of a stamp account does not make it at all certain that the depositor will continue to save after the ephemeral interest of holding stamps has lost its charm. The experience of the Provident Savings Bank has been that but a relatively small number of stamp depositors transfer their accounts to bank books.

Easy as it is, as has been shown, for any one to begin to save, and numerous as are

[1] "The Manual of School Savings Banks in the United States," with supplements, will be mailed on application to the editor of the *American Banker*, 29 Murray Street, New York, price fifty cents. The manual shows how a school bank may be most easily operated. It should be in the hands of every public school teacher.

the agencies of savings banks established in schools, churches, clubs, factories, workshops, and wholesale and retail stores, there is a class of people that is not reached by any one of these institutions, — a class to which no organization as a whole can make an effective appeal. To such, a personal appeal must be made by a collector that will go directly into the homes of the poor and will return to them as persistently as does the rent collector or the insurance agent. Such a one has been called a " wandering conscience," and he should be the untiring reminder to the poor of the fact that with themselves lies the remedy for many of the evils which degrade them. The savings collector must have a regular day for making a visit to a family, so that it may expect his coming and may feel the necessity of meeting his demand. He must be a rival of the insurance agent, who, with his insidious stories of the profits arising from the insuring of the lives of adults and children, makes a steady drain on the resources of the family. The Associated Charities of Boston reports that the Home Savings

Society "has been (*in some wards*) a successful competitor to the industrial insurance agent."

In England the system of *House to house collecting* has become so widespread that there are but few churches in London that do not have some form of collecting savings banks as a part of their parish work. The system has found its way into the rural districts, and in one small town of two hundred inhabitants the collector has been most successful, going from one isolated home to another and reaching people that but seldom have the gratification of receiving a visitor. One old woman used to welcome the collector by saying, "Yes, Miss, I'll give, if it's only for the sake of seeing some one once a week," and another received with surprise her accumulated savings, saying, "It's like a gift, only it's better than a gift; there's such a relish with it." This old woman, at least, had learned that she "must be her own benefactor" if she is "to value the gift."

The important rules that should be followed by any collecting savings bank are:—

1. That no interest be paid on the money held by the collectors, but that depositors be encouraged to transfer their savings to a bank as soon as $5, or possibly less, has been accumulated.

2. That, as has been said, the visits of the collector be paid at some fixed time, Monday morning, for instance, or as soon after pay day as is possible.

3. That the collector should realize that the system is merely a preparatory one for a higher form of saving, and that, therefore, no name be kept on his book simply because he has got into the habit of calling at a particular house and finds it pleasant to continue to make visits when he knows that payments are sure.

Most of the collecting societies are further regulated by the same rules that apply to the savings banks — such as that a week's notice be given before money can be withdrawn, that cards be presented in person to the bank, and that the amount represented on a lost card be forfeited. The Boston Home Savings Society requires that an order for money be

F

countersigned by the collector, and this rule
is also in force in the English societies.
Where the mere rudiments of saving are being taught and a family is only gradually
being taken from the class of dole receivers,
it is necessary that there should be some super-
vision of the spending of the savings. The
Associated Charities of Boston considers that
the growth of the Society has been extraordi-
nary, and that it is due not only to the energy
of the volunteer collectors, but to the fact that
there are many persons who, though able to
save, are too ignorant to make a beginning.
In one of the wards, where the work was be-
gun in 1887, the agent reports that one of the
first families to join the Society now owns a
house in the suburbs, and other agents report
that families that had been receiving public
and private aid now have their own savings-
bank accounts. One such family has $55
in bank; another has $36; and a third, $20.

A possible danger is that the collector may
be looked on as a dun, but to avoid this the
visitor must exercise judgment and tact.

The system is so simple that it can be introduced wherever there is a friend that wishes to visit the poor. Stamps may be got from the Penny Provident Fund or from any savings bank that uses the stamp system, a few responsible people can organize a society and begin work with a small board of managers, which shall appoint collectors and a treasurer.

In order to guard the interests of the poor, too great care cannot be taken in the choice of the collectors. The Orange Bureau of Charities has a paid collector, as have also the St. Paul Associated Charities and the Penny Provident Fund. It has been the experience of the last society that a paid collector is more successful than a volunteer, but it is a question whether he can carry to those on whom he calls the message of kindliness and fellowship that a good visitor can bear.

A less educational form of saving than those mentioned is that represented by coal clubs, flour clubs, etc., — less educational, first, because there is a certain paternalism in getting people to save money not to spend it themselves, but to have it spent for them; and secondly, because, though all such clubs are founded in order to teach economy and independence, they cannot attain their end so long as they give a bonus to those that save, by selling at less than cost price or by charging nothing for the necessary current expenses. As has been said in speaking of the collecting savings banks, this form of savings may be and is used as a preparation for higher forms of saving. It should, however, be carefully guarded against abuse, and the undue multiplication of these agencies in any community should be avoided. Such clubs have a tendency to make their members extravagant, because as the consumer does not buy the article he is using, he fails to realize its value. Indeed, these agencies are said to be inimical to thrift and seldom to serve as "stepping-stones on the way to stronger associations."

In Baltimore the Thomas Wilson Fuel Savings Society has done valuable work during the past seventeen years in teaching people to save in summer so as to buy coal for winter use. The Society has an endowment fund of $100,000, the interest on which covers the cost of operation and enables the Society to sell coal in winter at less than what it is bought for in summer.[1] The money for coal is deposited by the poor during the summer months, in small weekly sums. In Philadelphia, in addition to the Fuel Savings Society and other such organizations, which are governed by regulations very similar to those of the Thomas Wilson, is a coöperative coal club[2] which purposes to be more educational than those described. It charges each member a ten cent annual fee, and visitors go from house to house to collect the weekly sums deposited by the purchasers of the coal. The society is coöperative only in so far as it gives an opportunity to a number of people to buy coal in common at wholesale rates. If the members did their own buying and so controlled the finances, there would be real mutuality.

Flour clubs, boot and clothes clubs, are managed in very much the same way as the coal clubs, and are rarely businesslike enterprises.

[1] The management is trying to make the cost of the coal equal the selling price.

[2] Many workingmen's clubs have made arrangements by which the members are able through coöperation to buy coal at wholesale rates.

Much of the energy that is being expended on the formation of such organizations could most profitably be directed into more permanent forms of usefulness.

An interesting experiment in buying supplies at less than retail price is being conducted by the Wells Memorial Institute of Boston. The Institute makes arrangement with different large firms, so that its 1515 members are enabled to buy the necessities as well as many of the luxuries of life at a discount of from five to thirty per cent. The Institute also buys such supplies as coal, flour, tea, and coffee, which it sells to its members at wholesale prices. The saving to members last year by the buying of these articles from the Institute was $1048.72.

The Medical Aid Association of the Institute receives from its members monthly dues, — single persons, twenty-five cents; husband and wife, forty-two cents; husband, wife, and all children under eighteen years, fifty-nine cents, — in return for which it guarantees the services of a first-class physician in times of sickness. Arrangements are also made to give members medicines at cost price and to furnish the services of an oculist and a dentist at discount rates.

What effect the extension of such a system of buying and selling would have on the labor market, it is not possible to discuss here; but any one who should wish to inaugurate such a scheme must remember that he is putting himself into competition with the retail trade.

In considering the various phases of the savings bank system adapted to the needs of the poor, we have seen that there has been no demand made on the saver other than what is implied in the name. The bank has gone to the people and urged on them · the necessity of laying by for future wants; but it has not asked its depositors to concern themselves about its management. It is educational because it shows an improvident class the need of foresight; a thriftless body the utility of being frugal. It is educational because it teaches men to be independent, and trains children to recognize the power they have of accumulating a small capital.

Further than this it cannot and does not go. It reaches the individual as an individual, not as a member of an organization. There is, however, a higher form of saving, which goes further than the savings banks and trains its supporters to an understanding of business methods and to an appreciation of joint responsibility and mutual dependence. It creates a "consciousness of kind," a consciousness that will make the individual realize what are his duties as a member of a community, and that will gradually raise him to a higher social level. It does not work any revolution, it does not create suddenly any new force, but it must slowly affect the condition of those that are taught to help one another while helping themselves. Such is the work that should be and is done by building and loan associations, people's banks, and friendly societies, if the primary object of their existence is not lost sight of through the cupidity of individual members. It is hoped that it may be shown in the following chapters that the best of these associations do fulfil the hopes of their promoters.

CHAPTER IV

COÖPERATIVE SAVINGS AND BUILDING-LOAN
ASSOCIATIONS

THREE years ago in an address delivered at
Yale one of the justices of the United States
Supreme Court said that the building and
loan association is bringing together the
laborer and capitalist and is "strong to improve the condition of the wage-earner by
making him a persistent saver and ultimately
a capitalist," and that "it is teaching the capitalist to enter into the coöperative spirit with
the laborer."

The advocates of these associations claim
that there is no spirit of anarchism in Philadelphia, the city in which the movement to
organize building and loan companies had its
rise, and that in 1879[1] no one of the stock-

[1] The American Social Science Association reported that in
1878 the Philadelphia associations felt the pressure of the times
less than most business concerns.

holders joined in the great strike. They also allege that the only effect the panic of 1893 had on these associations was a temporary retarding of their growth, and they declare that they are now recognized as being a permanent and valuable economic feature of this country, and that their management has been so conservative that one-tenth of one per cent will fully cover the loss that was sustained by them between 1880-1890.   Whatever may or may not be claimed for such institutions, it is true that there are more than 6000 building and loan associations in the United States.   In the Ninth Annual Report of the United States Commissioner of Labor, it is shown that in 1893 there were 5838 associations in the United States, which had paid into them, as dues and interest on loans, $450,667,594 by 1,745,725 shareholders, one-fourth of whom were women.[1]   In a supplementary report[2]

[1] Ninth Annual Report of the Commissioner of Labor, 1893, "Building and Loan Associations," p. 14.

[2] Bulletin of the Department of Labor, No. 10, May, 1897, p. 370 *sq.*

it is stated that New York State has 383 societies, with 1,414,166 shares outstanding; Pennsylvania, 1131, with 1,796,311 shares outstanding; Illinois, 726, with 2,330,436 shares; Indiana, 502, with 814,811 shares; and Massachusetts, 119, with 461,913 shares.

These figures prove that whatever may be the effect or the tendency of what the English call an American experiment of " building up of homes for the people," the movement is one that has appealed to the workingman, and has had in this country greater success than any other form of coöperation.

The first building association was introduced into the United States from England in 1831, but it was not until the decade between 1840–1850 that the development of such societies became marked.

The various societies formed to give the workingmen of small incomes a safe place in which to deposit their surplus earnings and from which to draw their prospective savings, have been known as building associations, building and loan associations, savings funds and loan associations, homestead aid associations, coöperation savings and loan associations, co-operative banks, and coöperative savings and building-loan associations. The last name is the one that Mr. Seymour Dexter, an author-ity on the subject, considers most comprehen-sive, for it defines almost exactly the object of such associations. It is, however, as are the other titles, misleading in one particular, for it suggests that loans should be made only to encourage the buying of homes, though loans may be made for any legitimate busi-ness purpose.

In a limited space it is impossible to give an adequate description of the work of the "com-pulsory savings banks" or to draw even an outline of the various phases through which they have passed. The divergences between the different societies are great and important, these divergences having been caused by the varying needs of the different communities in which the organization has been founded, and by the operation of the laws of the forty-four states and territories that have passed special acts to govern the formation and the manage-ment of such societies. The many promoters of building associations have likewise had different conceptions of the scope of the institutions. All those, however, who have been disinterested in their efforts to organize a democratic institution, by means of which men mutually interested in providing for their future needs may find a safe and profitable place in which to deposit their surplus earnings and from which to borrow money to be repaid from future savings, have been guided by the cardinal principle that such associations must offer to the depositors and the borrowers, safety, equality, and simplicity. It is essential that every depositor should be assured of the safe keeping of his money, that he, whether borrower or non-borrower, should have an equal share of the profits and an equal right with other members to take part in the management of his association, and that he should be able to understand clearly the regulations that govern it. The observance of these fundamental rules will make sure that there shall be no preferred class and will assure to each member a full share of all the benefits — financial and educational — that the society can offer.

Owing to the great success of the local building and loan associations, there was formed in 1886, in Minneapolis, a *national association*, which has been the forerunner of 240[1] other associations of a like character.

These associations have a bad reputation because many of them have been mismanaged and are conducted in an expensive way; the cost of operating one of the large New York associations being over twenty per cent of receipts.[2] It is said in the report above mentioned, that the prejudice against National Associations is being overcome, and that as a rule they are conducting their business with integrity;[3] but even though their management be above reproach, they cannot be rivals for our consideration with the local societies; they must always expend a large proportion of their receipts for running expenses, and can never

---

[1] Report of the Commissioner of Labor, p. 14.

[2] The New York State League of Coöperative Savings and Building Loan Associations stated at its annual meeting, July, 1897, that the rate of expenses to assets as shown by the statistical table is: National, .39 %; locals, .08 %; or almost five to one.

[3] Report of the Commissioner of Labor, p. 16.

be in any real sense coöperative. That they do try to be national prevents them from being successful in bringing their membership into mutual relationship. The national coöperative building and loan associations are anomalies, because they are not and cannot be mutual in character or democratic and economic in management.

As Philadelphia is the city in which the building and loan movement had its rise and in which it has taken firmest hold, it is well to consider the *Philadelphia system* with some care. The origin of the plan was the realization of the fact that the poor man should by his own efforts become independent, and that as he could not, alone, command capital, he must call on his fellow-workmen to join with him to make small sums of money represent a large total. The influence of this mutual dependence of men whose small accumulations of savings represented, necessarily, much self-denial, could but have the effect of developing such civic virtues as neighborliness, sobriety, and morality, and such economic benefits as come from raising the standard of life by individual exertion.

The first step to be taken by a prospective building association is, therefore, the bringing together of men who live within a limited area of a city. After each has signed his name to a preliminary agreement, by which he binds himself to further the organizing of the society, he writes the number of shares to which he is willing to subscribe, and arranges with his co-workers to call a meeting for those who may wish to join the association in its initial stage. The only paid official should be the secretary, — the treasurer may be given a salary if the work be heavy, — and his compensation should be gauged by the amount of business he is called on to transact. The other officers should render gratuitous service, being actuated by a desire to make the association a practical success. It must be determined whether the shares are to be issued in series or simply in one series, and what number of shares each member is entitled to hold. As the terminating or single-issue plan necessitates that the association be dissolved when the shares mature, it is now generally superseded by the serial plan, which arranges for a reissue of shares either annually or semi-annually. In Philadelphia, the maturing value of a share is $200. If a man wish to become a member of an association that is just about to issue shares of the maturing value of $200, he will pay an initiation fee of 25 cents, to cover the cost of the pass-book, etc., and his first instalment of monthly dues, amounting to $1. If the man fail in his payment at any monthly meeting, he is fined 10 cents, or ten per cent of the amount due. Dividends are declared annually, semi-annually, or quarterly, but the profits, instead of being handed to him, are accredited to his account, so that his share may mature in 132 or 144 months. He will have to deposit therefore in monthly dues only about three-fifths of the face value of his share. If at any time he find it inconvenient to continue to meet the monthly payment of $1, he may, after giving thirty days' notice, withdraw his deposits, and will receive the full amount of his savings and a proportion of the accrued interest. Shares are transferable, a small fee — 25 cents per share — being charged by the

c

association for so doing.   The association never should, however, lose sight of its prime object, the loaning of money to members.   The money is sold at the monthly meetings, and each member has the right to borrow an amount equal in value to his matured share or shares.   As there may be more would-be borrowers than available capital, each successful borrower may have to pay a bonus for the privilege of getting a loan.   He that is willing to give the highest premium for the use of the money will become the successful borrower.   The question of the way in which the premium shall be charged against the borrower is one that has caused great discussion amongst the various associations, and it has been answered in many different ways.   A sound principle is that the premium should be looked on merely as a bonus given by the person that can make most profitable use of the money, and that, therefore, if there be no competition between the borrowers there be no premium charged.[1]

Every borrower must give as security for

[1] In some of the New York suburban towns associations have been lending money to the members without premium.

his loan not only the value of his matured share, but a first mortgage on real estate, or government or other bonds. In some cases, an assignment of the stock, on which there has been paid in more than the amount of the loan, is taken as security. It seems as if it were impossible for a workingman to give a mortgage on real estate as the security for a loan, until it is appreciated that the mortgage may be placed on the property that he buys with his borrowed capital. The very fact that he has bought a home gives the association the best possible assurance that he will do his utmost to meet his obligations. As soon as the loan is made, the borrower begins to cancel his indebtedness. He continues to pay his monthly dues on his unmatured share, in addition to which he pays interest on the loan, so that when the share matures, his debt is cancelled. He has never had to meet a day of reckoning, but by slowly accumulating small sums of money has met his monthly payments. No member may borrow more than a sum represented by the face value of his share or shares, so the matured value of the share must always be at least equal to the loan. A lesser sum than that represented by a share may be borrowed, and repayments may be made by instalments, so that the debt can be cancelled before the share has matured. As the share loans are one of the great factors in the usefulness of the associations, their value to members in helping them to meet some pressing need should never be lost sight of.

Only members are entitled to become borrowers, but as any reliable person may, in order to negotiate a loan, join an association by paying back dues on the last share issued by it,[1] there is no barrier offered to a man's becoming a member of an association for the purpose of raising money on good security.

Edmund Wrigley[2] gives the following table to show the cost to a workingman of buying a house by means of a building and loan association. He is supposed to have borrowed on six shares in order to buy a $1000 house, on which there is a $500 ground rent. As a

---

[1] An interest charge is sometimes levied on back dues. As new shares are issued at short intervals this charge is not heavy.

[2] "The Workingman's Way to Wealth," p. 59.

premium of twenty-five per cent was charged
for the loan, he received only $900.

Yearly ground rent or interest	$30.00
Taxes, etc. (about)	20.00
Yearly total of monthly dues and interest to the association at $12	144.00
Yearly interest on $100 advanced by himself	6.00
Total yearly expenses as owner	200.00
Former rent as tenant	180.00
Yearly difference	$20.00

According to this table he will become in
eight to eleven years the owner of the property, having made no further outlay than is
represented by the annual $20.   No mention
is made in Mr. Wrigley's calculation, however,
of the cost of repairs to the house, nor of the
character of the building; and the sum mentioned for taxes, etc., is smaller than is usual
on a house of such value.

Henry S. Rosenthal[1] gives the following
estimate of the cost of a $500 loan, dues $1
per week, dividends eight per cent per annum
on amount deposited, premium on loan 5 cents
per week, interest on loan six per cent per

[1] "Manual for Building Associations," p. 142.

annum, time required for payment, nine years
and twelve weeks : —

Total interest paid	$153.26
" premium "	24.00
" cost of loan	177.26
Total dues during 9 years, 12 weeks . .	480.56
Dividends	19.44
Credits . . .	$500.00

If a man be unable to meet his payments,
his mortgage is foreclosed, but according to
the Report of the Commissioner of Labor [1]
the total number of foreclosures for 5206
local associations was but 7765 ; total amount,
$11,031,394, loss to the associations, $441,106.
Though a man that is six months in arrears
for dues may be considered to have forfeited
his deposits, the directors are often very
lenient in settling the accounts of members
that have been unavoidably prevented from
meeting the payment of their dues.

The conditions necessary for the success of
an association such as has been outlined,
are, a community of wage-earners or persons

[1] " Report of the Commissioner of Labor," p. 306.

with small incomes, and an element of permanency in the local enterprises from which the incomes of the members are drawn. Reliable and devoted persons must be in charge, and care should be taken to make the expense of management 'small, so that the profits of the association, arising from interest on loans, premiums, fines, transfers, entrance fees, and profits on withdrawals, may go to the members.

To ensure the coöperation of the members, meetings should be held monthly, and at these meetings dues should be payable and loans made. The monthly meeting has been said to have somewhat 'of the educational value of .the New England town-meeting, but it is difficult to assure attendance, and the experience in many places is similar to that of the New York associations. In the city of New York at least one-half of the membership of all the associations is said to be indifferent to the management of their societies, and a society of three hundred members was unable recently to bring together more than three members, outside of the board of management, to make a radical change in the constitution.

The advantages of a system such as has been described are, that it gives each member a voice in the management of his association, that it makes it easy for persons of limited income to accumulate capital, and that it furnishes a safe place of dèposit for regular savings. Two additional points of special importance are, that it teaches the industrial classes how to manage their own property and gives them the power of securing in advance the benefit of their earnings.

This system is in favor in Philadelphia and New York, but in the West it has been superseded by the *Dayton plan*, which is said by its advocates to be much more comprehensive than the other system. According to the Dayton plan [1] a fresh series of stock may be issued at any time, so that a newly elected member need not be called on to pay back dues. Regular and uniform payment of dues is not required, and no fines are levied on the non-borrowers. For the convenience of

---

[1] It is said that a larger proportion of the population of Dayton belongs to building and loan associations than of any other city of the United States.

members the office is open at all times, and earnings are divided semi-annually and are subject to withdrawal. It is easy to see that each of these conditions must appeal to the members, and that the plan is more flexible and better adapted to meet the requirements of such persons as draw variable incomes. It lacks, however, the disciplinarian effect of the serial plan, and cannot be as educational. The building and loan associations can, moreover, never be the savings banks of persons that receive uncertain incomes, for it is essential that a member should have an approximate notion of what he will be able to save from month to month.

Building and loan associations are not rivals of the savings banks. Their functions are different and they appeal to a different class of savers. They should, however, be co-workers, the one encouraging the working-man to save, the other acting as a spur to thrift. The one meets the needs of the men that have fluctuating incomes and are likely to move from place to place; the other is ready to supply the demand of those that are drawing regular wages and are not likely to change their residences.

As the savings banks have a fixed debt the interest given by them is generally lower than that given by the building and loan associations, and the members of the latter are constantly lowering their indebtedness by the monthly instalments received on the loans. The repayment of the loans is assured because the homes of the borrowers are given as security. The successful management of a savings bank depends more on skilful investments than does that of a building association, and it must hold a larger reserve fund. There can be no run on a building and loan association, for the constitution of each declares that no loans are made in excess of a certain per cent of all the paid-in capital, and all loans have to be cancelled by the matured shares, so that in a well-managed association there must be a sufficient fund on hand to pay off the matured shares.

The risk of belonging to such associations lies in the fact that they may be managed by a class of persons that has but small business experience. It may, therefore, be easy

for a few crafty speculators to get control of
the savings of a confiding body of workingmen. It has also been said that they tend
to make labor immobile. In a country where
there is constant change in the methods of
production, caused by the evolution of machinery, the workingman may need, in his
effort to get work, to change his locality, and
may find it a disadvantage to be tied down
by the ownership of a house. If this argument were to be logically applied, it would
tend to discourage the ownership of property
in any community, and would make a large
body of workingmen mere rolling stones.
Whatever may be the possible dangers inherent in the system, and carefully as such
dangers should be guarded against, an institution that encourages men to help themselves
is a valuable one. It is a great incentive to
a man who must live on the margin of a bare
livelihood to feel that he can, by taking weekly
or monthly a small sum from his regular
wages, provide for a probable future need, or
gradually buy a house by letting his association be his rent collector until he has freed

his homestead from debt. Then in his middle or old age he will have learned to appreciate the motto of the United States league of building and loan associations, — "The American home, the safeguard of American liberties."

Before a building and loan association is started in any community, the promoter should carefully consider whether or not there is already in the town or city in which he lives a sufficient number of associations to meet the demand. In many places the success of these societies has caused an uncalled for increase in their number, so that consolidation is needed to ensure healthy growth. One point further may be mentioned, which is, that in questioning the status of any society, it is very important to find out whether the accounts are audited regularly by competent business men (many states require that the associations be examined annually or biennially by state officials), and whether the attorney is an experienced lawyer.

The annual reports and the constitution and by-laws of such organizations as the Workingmen's Coöperative Bank of Boston, the presi-

dent of which is Mr. Robert Treat Paine, the
Englewood Mutual Loan and Building Association of Englewood, New Jersey, and The
Thrift, a Savings and Loan Fund of Brook-
lyn, New York, can give valuable aid to such
persons as wish to help the workingman to
form similar associations.   The associations
mentioned, and many others, prove that philanthropic energy may be directed towards
helping workingmen to get their own homes
by a safe and easy investment of regular
savings.

There is one loan association that needs to
be specially mentioned because it differs in
several particulars from any class that has
been described. The Dime Savings and Loan
Association of Indianapolis, whose first president was Mr. Oscar C. McCulloch, was organized in 1887. It was established so as to be
an adjunct to the work of the Charity Organization Society of Indianapolis, and was intended
to combine "all the features of a savings bank,
all the benefits of a building association." No
fines were to be exacted for non-payment of
weekly dues and no withdrawal fees were to

be charged. A large balance was to be kept in the bank for the use of the non-borrowers, who might wish to draw on their savings without giving notice, and each member was to be entitled to borrow a sum equal to the face value of his share, repayments for which should be made at the rate of twenty-five cents a week for each sum of $100 or fraction thereof, unless a higher premium than ten per cent had been bid for the use of the loan. If more than ten per cent were charged, a proportional increase in the weekly instalments would have to be met. The value of each share was to be $25, weekly dues ten cents. The association has practically made but little effort to encourage borrowing, the amount that has been loaned on real estate having been only $3,052.27. The special feature of the work of the society is the method of collecting the dues. The Charity Organization Society employs a collector at its own cost, to go in a buggy from house to house to receive the savings of the members of the Dime Savings and Loan Association. The collector is able to make as many as 223 visits a day — the average is about 175 — and to collect dues varying in amount from ten cents to $1. One of his reports shows that he collected in one day $25.87 from 101 persons, and that he accepted any amount of money that was offered him, no stress being laid on the fact that the nominal weekly dues of the society are ten cents. It has been a great surprise to the association that "the more· stringent the times, the greater effort the people make to save," and during the continued business depression of the past three years, the subscriptions have been steadily increasing.

Some months ago an effort was made to have the depositors come to the office, but it was unsuccessful.

Dr. E. R. L. Gould, in an article on the "Economics of Improved Housings,"[1] says, that though "coöperative building and loan associations have rendered most valuable individual and social service . . . they present three leading drawbacks." First, the expense to the borrower is greater than need be, the

[1] *Yale Review*, May, 1896.

lender getting enhanced profits at the expense of the borrower; secondly, business skill of a high order is not always available for the management; and thirdly, that if the borrower die before his term payments are completed, his family is often obliged to surrender the property at a financial loss. A scheme that is said in this article to be "the cheapest, fairest, and most effective" ever carried into practice is one very similar to that now being tried by the *City and Suburban Homes Company of New York City*. The main features of the plan are based on an experiment that has been successfully made in Belgium. In 1889 was passed in that country a laborers' dwelling act [1] which gives to the General Savings Bank, a semi-official institution, the authority to loan at a reduced rate a part of its reserve to local building and loan associations. The law also provides for the creation of committees of patronage, which are appointed in each district as semi-official bodies on good works "to encourage the development of

[1] Eighth Special Report of the Department of Labor, "Housing of the Working People," pp. 133-152.

thrift and of life insurance as well as loan companies and mutual relief and pension funds." The most important feature of the law, and the one that has been introduced into this country by the management of the City and Suburban Homes Company, is "the institution of life insurance in connection with the repayment of loans."

The City and Suburban Homes Company does not act as the agent of any national or private bank, nor are its operations supervised by any officially appointed committee, but as has been said it has adopted, as an essential feature of its work, the principle that all payments for a home shall be rendered certain, even in the event of the death of the purchaser before his instalments have been completed, by making it compulsory for every successful applicant to write an insurance policy. This company was organized in 1896 with a capital stock of $1,000,000, divided into $10 shares.[1] Five per cent dividends are

[1] The capital stock is now $2,000,000, and the average price of the cottages already sold is about $3100. "This includes cost of land, buildings, grading, paving, curbing, macadamizing, sewers, and all improvements."

H

guaranteed to the stockholders, and any further
profits that accrue after meeting this charge
and that of the reserve fund, ten per cent, go
to the improvement of the property.   It is
hoped that workingmen, especially those that
are purchasing homes of the company, will
become shareholders.   The houses owned by
the company are divided into two classes, city
tenements and suburban cottages.   It is the
latter class that is of peculiar interest to us.
The homes vary in cost from $1000 to $2000,
and are built so as to be suited to the needs
of workingmen and clerks that receive salaries
of from $800 to $1500 a year.   If after careful investigation an applicant is found to be
satisfactory, morally, mentally, and physically,
his name is enrolled on a waiting list, and
after one hundred eligible applications have
been made, a lot of ground is chosen and
specifications are handed to each prospective
buyer.   If possible, an applicant pays in cash
ten per cent of the purchase money, if not,
he is enabled to borrow the necessary sum
from the National Surety Company of New
York.   Each purchaser must take a life insur-

ance policy for twenty years reserve settlement, and this policy is payable to the company if he die before the payments on the house have been completed. As the policy has a cash surrender value after premiums have been paid on it for three years, the company can partly reimburse itself if there be any default in the payments on its property. The buyer is given the option of completing his payments on his house within ten, fifteen, or twenty years, but the last length of time is considered the wisest as it gives a man drawing a small salary a sufficient time in which to meet his obligations. The full charge for the property includes instalments of the principal, interest on deferred payments, and life insurance premiums, which are payable monthly, and, as has been calculated, should not, including cost for taxes and repairs, exceed twenty-five per cent of a man's income, based on a salary of $1000 per annum. The buying of homes by young men is encouraged, as the cost for insurance is less for them than for older buyers, and they are assured that if the necessity should arise for their changing their residence on account of the exigencies of labor, the company will make an equitable settlement with them.   In the event of a man's death, any surplus that may be left after the charges against his policy have been met, is handed to his family; but if he live till the payments are completed, he has, in addition to his un- encumbered house, a life insurance policy that will assure him either an annuity in old age or an adequate death benefit for the use of his heirs.   Great care is taken to prevent any speculating on the part of the purchasers, and without the consent of the company, no sub- letting or renting of the property is permitted.[1]

The first site selected by the company for its suburban cottages is Homewood,[2] a tract of 530 lots within six miles of the City Hall.

The workings of the company can be in- definitely extended, for they need to be limited only by the number of eligible applications. This system is one that may be introduced into any large city, and the growth of the

[1] See "New York's Great Movement for Housing Reform," *Review of Reviews*, December, 1896.

[2] See "Homewood," a model suburban settlement, *Review of Reviews*, July, 1897.

New. York plan should be carefully watched,
therefore, by all philanthropists that are interested in the great question of how to provide
better homes for the people.   Even though
better housing has a direct relation to thrift, it
is not possible here to speak in greater detail
of the admirable work that is being done in this
direction in some of our large cities, but attention may be called to one other scheme which
seems to call forth the savings of the small
wage-earner.   In 1896 the East Side Settlement of New York City organized a *Coöperative House Owning and Industrial Company*, to
give to citizens living in flats an opportunity
of owning their homes.   As in the City and
Suburban Homes Company, the shares were
but $10, and these were payable in instal-
ments, and might be subscribed to by the
tenants of the company as well as by other
workingmen.

CHAPTER V

In discussing the coöperative savings and building-loan associations we have seen that they differ from the savings banks in three important points: they are managed by the class that invests in them, they make saving compulsory, and they make it easy and profitable for their members to borrow. Statistics, however, show that in spite of this last inducement, only one-fourth [1] of the members of these associations are borrowers. The borrower in the majority of cases uses his loan to purchase a house, and though he is gradually relieving himself from the demands made on his income by a landlord, and will, when his share matures, have become possessed of property that is only encumbered by the necessary outlay for taxes

[1] Per cent of borrowers in associations reporting, 26.25; local, 29.83; national, 13.77. Report of the Commissioner of Labor, 1893, "Building and Loan Associations," p. 15.

and repairs, he is not making his money reproduce itself. Such societies do not therefore
make a very large number of capitalists, and
are only in a small measure recruiting the
capitalistic class from beneath.

The People's Banks of Germany and Italy
are really making their members not only the
holders of their own savings, but their own
bankers and financiers. They are teaching
the poor to look on savings not as a mere pos-
session, but as "an implement of work," and
on money as an article that is "well worth
hiring at a price." They differ in two very
important particulars from our building and
loan associations, for they reach a poorer
class of people, and they do business mainly
with borrowed capital instead of confining
their operations to the lending or the investing of capital furnished by the membership.[1]
The aims of the banks are: economic — to
enable the economically weak to make themselves financially strong by the power of com-
bination; moral — to bring neighbors together

[1] "Coöperative Credit Associations in Certain European
Countries," United States Department of Agriculture, p. 112.

by teaching them the community of interests, and to develop character by showing the need of self-restraint; educational — to train in business methods and in the appreciation of the value of money. In the most natural way the economic instincts are appealed to first, and on the foundation of material interests is built a firm superstructure. The objects of the banks are: to extend the leading forms of coöperation; to make "association a means whereby credit may be got on reasonable and easy terms by persons who individually could obtain it, if at all, only on difficult and usurious conditions";[1] and to borrow money in order that it may be lent to the members.

In establishing people's banks the cardinal rules have been: "Maximum of responsibility, minimum of risk, maximum of publicity." To secure the first, unlimited liability has been accepted by the members; to secure the second, the membership has been carefully guarded and the banks have been allowed to invest in no speculative enterprises; to assure the third, the actions of the banks have been

[1] "Coöperative Credit Associations," p. 21.

made public and the membership has been confined to a district within which each member can be well known by every other member.

It is believed that an enduring union of forces is better secured by the creating of security than by the mere bringing together of "driblets of means." Since, therefore, the moral standing of each member is considered much more important to the bank than his financial, his trustworthiness is brought in question rather than his money worth, his intrinsic rather than his extrinsic value to his community. The reliability of a borrower is the fundamental consideration, because the essential feature of the system is the establishment of the policy of repayment. There must be "Vigilance, careful examination alike of the borrower and of loans; enforcement of conscientious application and conscientious repayment of the money lent." The result of the enforcement of these simple rules has been that the industrious poor have been proved to be as good creditors as the rich, and in localities where there seemed to be no penny of ready money has mysteriously come forth sufficient capital to create new industries, and to restock and refertilize the impoverished soil. In reading Mr. Wolff's fascinating book on people's banks [1] we feel as if he were describing the work that has been done by some good genius, until by the accumulation of evidence we learn that no power has been at work other than that which teaches people to help themselves and to avail themselves of the opportunities that lie at their doors.

The great pioneers of the people's bank movement in Germany were Schulze-Delitzsch and Raiffeissen. They severally appreciated that any system to be successful must be shaped to meet the needs of the class among which it is applied. They knew that coöperation is something higher than mere working together; that real coöperation means a willingness to

[1] "People's Banks: A Record of Social and Economic Success," by Henry W. Wolff. P. S. King & Son, London, 1896. In this chapter the author has made numerous quotations from Mr. Wolff's book. It is recommended that those who are interested in the subject read "People's Banks" in full, and that any one who may contemplate inaugurating such banks read, also, his small manuals: "Village Banks" and "A People's Bank Manual." P. S. King & Son, London; price, twenty cents each.

subordinate personal advantage to the general good; and that if coöperation is to become an economic force it must have some higher ideal than mere economic gain — it must be inspired by an ethical motive.

The first Raiffeissen loan bank was founded in 1849 in a little German village, and not until five years later was a second founded. In 1862 was a third venture made, but by 1891 the number of these banks in Germany had grown to be 885. In 1893, the year of the terrible drought, they proved their great usefulness by the way in which they came to the assistance of the distressed husbandmen, to whom they were able to render more practical help than was the State itself. In 1896 their number was 2169, and they could personally boast that " Neither member nor creditor has ever lost a penny " through us.[1]

In the formation of such banks the first con-

[1] Mr. C. R. Henderson, in "The Social Spirit in America," p. 158, says, "In forty-three years no member or creditor (of a Raiffeissen loan bank) has lost a cent," and Dr. Ely considers it "doubtful if in America any one kind of business can show so small a proportionate number of failures as the Coöperative German Unions." "Coöperative Credit Associations," p. 45.

sideration is whether each member is reliable. The members as a body, as well as individually, are interested in protecting the moral standard of their bank, because they know that each is pledged to share the burden of loss thrown by a defaulting member on the bank. To assure a thorough knowledge of the moral standing of every member, the operations of the bank must be confined to a limited district, and each application for membership must be carefully scrutinized. No distinction is recognized between the different members, but it has been found advisable to have a few rich men in each bank, and as they have to bear the brunt of the liability, they have often been given a principal part in the administration. A rich man may help a rural bank by contributing a small gift toward the expense of starting and by making deposits so as to attract other savers; but his chief usefulness can lie in sharing the common liability and by taking part in the administration, provided no spirit of patronage be introduced and the "cardinal principle" of the bank, equality, be maintained.[1]   The council of such

[1] See "Village Banks," pp. 15, 16.

a bank is composed of volunteer workers, the
only paid officer being the cashier, to ensure
whose honest discharge of his duties a frequent
and careful auditing of the accounts is required.
In the formation of these banks it was fully
realized that the poor man has "no credit because he is destitute, and he is destitute because
he has no credit," therefore the only pledge he
can give of his reliability is his labor. As they
were intended to reach those who had neither
credit nor cash, they issued no shares and had
no entrance fee.

Now, owing to legislative enactment, it is
required that such associations issue shares,
but the amount of each share is so small that it
does not debar any one from membership. It
was, also, the purpose of the founder that there
should be no dividends, because the declaring of
dividends might tempt shareholders to charge a
high interest for the use of their money, and so
confute the object of the establishment of the
banks. The banks are now required to declare
dividends, but, instead of enriching the shareholders, the dividends are placed in a reserve
fund, and so strengthen the banks and lessen the

liability of the members. If the reserve fund should become unnecessarily large, a part of it may be used for some public service. It can be seen that there is little temptation to charge borrowers a high rate of interest, the rate having to be determined only by the amount that the bank has to pay for the use of money borrowed by it. The difference need be great enough only to meet the cost of administration and of accumulating a small reserve fund. One advantage of these mutual credit banks must not be lost sight of, *i.e.* that they are most valuable depositories for the savings of their members.

From what has been said, it would seem that borrowing is made easy, but such is not the case. The principle on which all loans is made is that the money be used for some productive purpose, not for " stopping a hole." The borrower must clearly state, therefore what is the use that he intends to make of his loan, and he is obliged to use the money in the way he has indicated. He gives a note of hand, generally indorsed by one or more securities, and he is required to pay interest and principal promptly.

In rural districts it is found that a longer time must be allowed for the repayment of a loan than in cities. Fifteen per cent of the loans of the Raiffeissen banks are granted for one year or less, forty-three per cent for from one to five years, thirty-four per cent for from five to ten years, and eight per cent for a longer period of time. If the loan were made to repair some failure through loss by accident, such as damage to buildings or to crops, repayment may be expected in two years; if to purchase live stock, in three years; and if to acquire land, or to build, in eight years.

If the council feel at any time that the loan is not being well used, the money may be called in; but if, on the contrary, it is being productively used, the time for which it was granted may be extended. No one feels a hesitancy in speaking of the mismanagement of a member that has it in his power to bring discredit on his bank or loss to it, so there is no difficulty in getting persons to check the use the individual makes of his loan.

These banks have had no difficulty in getting sufficient money to meet the demands made on them. What is needed, in excess of the savings or other deposits, is raised by borrowing from non-members. Their credit is so good that they find it easy to borrow either from individuals or from public banks. In 1866 and 1870, the years of the Austro-Prussian and the Franco-Prussian wars, deposits were withdrawn from other banks to be "pressed on the Raiffeissen banks for safe keeping."

The increasing number of banks led to the organization of a central bank, which "derives its strength from the local association," and encourages the formation of new banks. Coöperative insurance, and coöperative dairies, coöperative hop and vine growing, and coöperative buying and selling of farm products, have been encouraged by the banks, which are especially ready to furnish money for the use of any such enterprises. In 1893, 610[1] Raiffeissen associations had 17,720,871 marks ($4,217,567.30) outstanding in loans, 3,068,334 marks ($873,063.49) advanced in cash credits,[2]

---

[1] "People's Banks," p. 134.

[2] Loans in "account current," which are of great practical use to the members.

473,758 marks ($112,754.40) in share capital,
1,176,389 marks ($279,980.58) in reserve fund,
and 24,620,600 marks ($5,859,702.80) in savings
deposits. The expenses for management were
240,905 marks ($57,335.39) for the 610 banks,
or about $94 each.

The different conditions that surround the
population of the large and of the small centres
have made it necessary to vary the regulations
that control the banks. In the country districts the borrowers are less educated than in
the cities, and need the money for a longer
period; in the cities the management has to
be left more to the directors than in the country, for in the former it is impossible to bring
the stockholders together, and it is not, therefore, as easy to watch the loans. In a crowded
community it is not possible to know your
neighbor as well as in a sparsely settled one,
the citizen is not so ready, therefore, to accept
unlimited liability as is the countryman. The
liability of each member of a city bank must
be limited to his number of shares.

The Schulze-Delitzsch banks, to reach a
different class of people, generally a more

I

moneyed class, had to solve the problem of banks for the people in a different way from that in which it had been solved by Raiffeissen. The first of its two principal objects, that money be borrowed from non-members for the use of members, is identical with that of the rural banks; but the second, that savings be encouraged by requiring members to take shares (on the instalment plan), is opposed to their spirit. When Schulze-Delitzsch died in 1883, there were 4000 associations organized in Germany according to his rules, which had 1,200,000 members. According to statistics collected in 1895, in 1047 associations of this type, there were 509,723 members; total paid-up share capital, $30,128,115; accumulated reserve, $8,794,560, in addition to the working capital of $114,433,820 raised by loans.[1]

In a small German village of 1500 population is a bank with a membership of 240.

---

[1] " People's Banks," p. 113. Mr. Wolff's statistics are too numerous to quote at length, but to get an adequate conception of the workings of the Schulze-Delitzsch Credit Associations it is necessary to read them in full.

Its capital is $7000, annual expenses $250.
One of the three officers is the school-
master, whose salary from the bank is $75.
The amount loaned and in actual use is
between $15,000 and $20,000 a year, which
does not include cash credits that are not
availed of.

In Italy the people's banks have been won-
derfully successful and have done an immense
amount of good. Signor Luigi Luzzatti,[1] the
introducer of people's banks into Italy, organized his first bank in Milan in 1866 with a
capital of $140. He had been moved to un-
dertake such a work because he felt that a
"war with usury" must be declared in Italy
as it had been in Germany, and that the way
to make such a warfare triumphant was to
call the people about him. He asked for
their savings, and said he could make his
banks independent of outside capital by at-
tracting "local deposits and local savings."
He did not believe, as did Schulze-Delitzsch,
that steady savings are dependent on the size of
the shares, and accordingly issued shares of the

[1] Signor Luzzatti was afterwards made Minister of Finance.

value of $5 to $10 each,[1] besides making his
entrance fees small.   He made use of the
experience that had been gained by his German forerunners, taking great care in the
selection of his members, and requiring, also,
that full and regular reports of the operations
of the banks should be rendered.   Feeling
that "responsibility must be made acute, effective, and general," he urged that all unreliable members be expelled.

The management of the Italian banks is in
the hands of a large volunteer council of responsible members.   A carefully selected committee keeps a table of the financial standing
of each member, and calculates from it what
is his borrowing value and the worth of his
securities.   If this committee find that a borrower has lowered his economic standing, the
council forces him to give better security; if
a surety lose his property, the borrower has to
furnish a substitute.   In addition to this committee is one that keeps an account of all
outstanding loans, and notes whether members

[1] Some of the shares of the Schulze-Delitzsch Credit Associations were as high as $125.

are tardy or punctual in their repayments.
Mortgages are seldom accepted as security,
for the banks do not wish to become burdened
with property of which it may be difficult to
dispose. Loans are usually granted for a
period of three months, and, except to agricul-
turalists, the lending of money for a greater
length of time is avoided, — all loans may,
however, be renewed.

A mistake made by some of these banks
has been to offer the shares for sale at a
premium, the reason for so doing being that
the large reserve fund increases the value of
the shares. The size of the reserve fund
should be limited by making the aggregate of
the loans smaller and by reducing the interest
charge. It should never be forgotten that
the great object of the bank is — to reach
the people. Some of the Italian banks have
offered "loans of honor" to persons that could
give neither surety nor security. Great care
is taken in the selection of the persons to
whom such loans shall be made, the banks
sometimes asking the friendly societies, the
so-called mother of the Italian people's banks,

to act as their agent in the distributing of the fund. So careful has been the investigation that the banks have had to bear but few losses from these loans of honor. The surplus funds of the banks are used, also, in making grants for technical education, or, as in Germany, in encouraging public works by financial gifts.

The bank of Milan, in which Signor Luzzatti said that "half his heart was wrapped up," is now "lodged in a palace," — a phrase which means less in Italy than in other countries, — and has a membership of 17,860. Between 130 and 140 volunteers and 100 paid clerks conduct the business. The paid-up capital is now 8,598,300 lire ($1,659,471.90); the number of shares, 171,966; reserve fund, 4,299,-150 lire ($829,735.95); deposits, 105,702,870; lire ($20,400,653.91).[1] During 1895, loans to the amount of 175,587,916 lire ($33,888,467.79) were made.

A former secretary of the bank says that the success of the *Banca Popolare* is owing to the "gratuitous rendering of services by the officers, the non-limitation of its capital, the

[1] "People's Banks," p. 217.

smallness of the payments exacted, the restriction of each member to one vote, the refusal of confidence to every member who has shown himself undeserving of it, the preference given to credit services over profit, and the exclusion of any hazardous operations." It must be borne in mind that this bank started in 1866 with a capital of $140.

In the poorest quarter of Florence is a small bank that was founded with a capital of $75, which has never reached more than $750. The value of each share is ten lire, payable in ten months. In this bank $5600 was deposited the first year, and $6200 was loaned, the profit on the latter being $600.[1]

In 1893 there were 730 Luzzatti banks,[2] 662 of which had a membership of 405,341. About seventy per cent of the loans were for sums ranging from $40 to $1000. The rate of interest has been high, from six per cent to eight per cent per annum.[3]

As in Germany, so also in Italy, it was felt

[1] " People's Banks," p. 234.   [2] *Ibid.*, p. 243.

[3] Six hundred and ninety-seven of these banks had 118,228,-000 lire ($22,818,004) in paid-up capital and reserve fund. *Ibid.*, p. 243.

that there should be a different type of bank
to meet the needs of the country folk from
that which was offered to the dwellers in the
cities, and in Italy as in Germany there was
a man to undertake the work. Signor Leone
Wollenborg felt the need of combating the
usurer on his own ground as keenly as did
Signor Luzzatti. He might in the words of
Robert Louis Stevenson have described the
condition of the people he strove to rescue
from the usurers: "But the Jew storekeepers
of California, profiting at once by the needs
and habits of the people, have made themselves in too many cases the tyrants of the
rural population. Credit is offered, is pressed
on the new customer, and when once he is
beyond his depth, the tune changes, and he
is from thenceforth a white slave. 'I believe,
even from the little I saw, that Kelmar, if
he chose to put on the screw, could send half
the farmers packing in a radius of seven or
eight miles round Calistoga. These are con-
tinually paying him, but are never suffered
to get out of debt. He palms dull goods upon
them, for they dare not refuse to buy; he

goes and dines with them when he is out on an outing, and no man is loudlier welcomed; he is their family friend, the director of their business, and, to a degree elsewhere unknown in modern days, their king." [1]

In founding his banks Dr. Wollenborg made the people understand that no one could become a member who was unable to read and write. The consequence has been that education has been encouraged. As he closes his door to the drunkard, dissipation has decreased; and as he withholds the privileges of the banks from a dishonest person, a premium is put on honesty.

There are now eighty-four village banks [2] organized according to his system, and only one of these banks has issued shares. Some have as much as $7500 outstanding in loans and an average deposit of $862. Their reserve fund does not average more than $65. [3] The interest taken by the members in their

---

[1] " The Silverado Squatters."

[2] There are nearly four hundred rural banks of independent formation in addition to those of the Wollenborg type.

[3] " People's Banks," pp. 268, 269.

banks is so great that it is easy to get a full attendance on meetings and to make the selection of new members judiciously.

The effect of the people's banks in Italy has been to lessen the number of depositors in the post-office savings banks, the people greatly preferring to use their own rather than the State's banking facilities. Their great success lies in the very fact that the people appreciate that they have created these banks — that they are their own.

As Mr. T. Mackay says : " Mr. Wolff proves beyond a shadow of doubt that in Germany and Italy, coöperative banking has rescued the poor from the extortionate money-lender and is now transacting a business counted in millions and on principles as safe, nay, even safer, than the Bank of England."

Unfortunately it is not possible, owing to lack of space, to give even a bald outline of what has been done in Austria, France, Belgium, and other European countries to further the organization of people's banks.[1]   It is to

[1] In "Coöperative Credit Associations" may be found interesting statistics, showing what has been done by people's banks,

be hoped, however, that what has been said will induce those interested in the subject to read Mr. Wolff's books. If it be once realized what a power for good is this method of enlarging the opportunities of the poor, there is no doubt that in this country will be found worthy imitators of Schulze-Delitzsch and Luzzatti, of Raiffeissen and Wollenborg. ·

If this credit system is to be applied successfully, it must be given a locality in which there is a people that is "willing and able to be industrious." It will not be fair, however, to judge of a community unless it be put to some practical test, for there is often, in an apparently moribund vicinage, vitality which does but need the tonic of new opportunities and fresh incentives.

There is a great advantage in a system such as we have been considering in that it immediately returns to the people from whom they are drawn the savings that have been slowly accumulated by them. It often, too, liberates

and in many of our magazines may be found recent articles on the subject.

capital and brings into productive use money that otherwise would be lying idle.

The success of such a system is dependent, as we have seen, on the care with which the members scrutinize the smallest details of the business, and study the condition of each borrower. No pains must be spared to make the workings of the bank thorough, and every member must have the right to examine the financial status of his association. Any interference on the part of the government or of any individual will be inimical to the success of the banks, because they are a plant that is killed by patronage and can only thrive when free to put out shoots, independent of any artificial stimulus.

The result of the establishment of people's banks has been found to be a raising of the moral standard of the communities in which they are organized; accordingly they are encouraged by the clergy of Germany, Italy, and other countries, who see that a new bond is drawing neighbors together, and that as the value of money is realized, less is spent at taverns and gambling-houses. When honesty is found to have a market price, its value appreciates.

In the small rural districts where the farmer has been unable to add to the productiveness of his land because of lack of ready money, such banks come as a godsend. Not only may he buy cheaper because of having ready money, but he may increase his stock, fertilize his soil, introduce improved machinery, and rebuild his barns, so that when the loan falls due he will, the productivity of his property having been enlarged, have more than enough out of the increase in his earnings with which to meet his payment. The element of time is peculiarly beneficial in one class of loans furnished by the foreign banks, — the "discounting of rents due." A small tenant may have his rent fall due just at a time when it is most inconvenient to pay it, and the landlord may need his rent before pay-day; the bank, by acting as intermediary, gives the former time to meet his obligations, and the latter the use of his rentals when the money can be most helpful. One of the great problems of the age, how to prevent the overpopulation of congested centres, may be in a measure solved, not by forcing the city poor into the country, but by adding to the chances an ambitious farmer's son has of succeeding on his own soil. If hard-worked and overstrained farmers are given the means of acquiring credit, they should be able to increase the producing power of their land.[1] It must be that in this country, as in Europe, the money will be forthcoming, if the right means be taken to bring it into circulation. May not some of the energy that has gone into offering potato patches and other palliatives for the use of the poor be directed into teaching the people how to help themselves without the introduction of any " little Providence " ?

In the cities the usefulness of such banks is no less great, for there too may be found many working men and women, who, lacking ready money, cannot make the most of their small talents. Might not a power to command credit do something toward taking the

[1] The coöperative loan associations of the United States " have rarely extended any part of their business into the rural districts." " Coöperative Credit Associations," p. 7.

poor from under the control of the sweating system? But whether or not they be relieved from the oppression of the sweater, each one of us knows of many cases where a little ready money would have enabled a man to set up in business for himself, or increase the profits of his present business. There are in several of our large cities societies formed to lend money to the poor on easy terms, but such societies do not reach them as does a mutual association. A man will be more scrupulous about the repayment of a loan when its non-payment means a loss that has to be borne by his friends, than when it has to be borne by an organization with which he has no affiliation. The careful consideration of the ability and the moral standing of each candidate for a loan, by persons who have an intimate acquaintance with the borrower, prevents the loan's being injudiciously made, either to a fraudulent person or to one who cannot turn his money to good account.

There are dangers inherent in the very success of these banks, but these dangers must be carefully guarded against by limiting the size of the shares, by declaring no dividends or very small dividends, by watching zealously the interest of the borrowers rather than that of the stockholders, by letting each bank be thoroughly in touch with its locality, and by making each study the peculiar needs of the district in which it is founded. With Schulze-Delitzsch each bank should cordially hate the dividend hunter, and each should realize that its success is dependent on prompt repayment. Prompt repayment should be the watchword of the people's banks.

One thing, however, must not be lost sight of, which is that the success of the associations is dependent on, and always must be dependent on, their being founded on a real coöperative basis. Coöperation does not mean, as has been said, a mere working together, but something deeper, nobler than that. The organizers of coöperative banks must therefore be moved by a spirit of altruism, and must be ready to sacrifice personal interests for the general good, must have "consideration for the consumer," and a generous recognition of the rights of each individual.

If such be the spirit of the founders of people's banks or of any other coöperative body, thrift and generosity will be taught together, foresight and prudence will not exclude openhandedness.

It is impossible in this manual to touch on the coöperative movement in America or on what is being done for the workingman by the advocates of profit sharing; but as in Germany, so in this country, may people's banks be found to be powerful auxiliaries of coöperative consumption and production, and ready combatants of socialism. The development of self-help will be found to kill the socialistic spirit.

May the time come, also, when the philanthropist will be able to say from his own experience,—

"Wer Raiffeissenvereine baut,
Reisst Armenhäuser nieder."[1]

[1] He who builds Raiffeissen banks destroys the almshouses.

K

CHAPTER VI

PROVIDENT LOAN ASSOCIATIONS

OPPOSED to the direct methods of saving that have been described, is what has been called the "inverse method," or that which offers to the poor loans of money to meet some temporary emergency.[1] A loan association, *per se*, may be considered to be opposed to thrift, for persons cannot be made "better inclined to thriftiness by increasing their power to borrow," unless, as has been shown in the preceding chapter, the object in borrowing money has been to use credit for some productive purpose.

If the promoters of provident loan associations had had merely to consider whether it were advisable to give people of small and fluctuating incomes an opportunity to borrow money on chattel mortgages, their problem would have been a simple one. But it was

---

[1] For exceptions see pp. 125, 126.

made complex by the necessity they felt of
rescuing the small borrower from the pawnbrokers, a class of men that is ever ready to
lend money, though in return for its services an
interest is charged that means the thrusting of
the defenceless borrower into a slough of indebtedness from which he is powerless to extri-
cate himself.   In all our large cities may be
found a body of usurers that are able to extort
from the borrower interest as high as, and often
higher than, ten per cent a month, and to them
the poor will and must apply unless the philanthropist is ready to offer a better way by which
money can be procured.

In a report made to the Citizens' Permanent
Relief Committee of Philadelphia in 1894, the
case of an electrician is cited, who had, until he
lost his position on account of illness, been able
to support his family comfortably.   After his
savings were exhausted he borrowed $50 from
a loan company, and gave as security "a judgment note and bill of sale on his furniture."
The loan was to be repaid in "thirteen weekly
instalments of $5.10 each."   After he had paid
$35.70, he was unable to meet his weekly in-

stalments, and was, therefore, threatened with "a sheriff's levy on his goods." The electrician's dilemma was brought to the notice of a man that had been carefully investigating such cases of usury, and by his intervention the company was forced to accept merely the amount due on the original loan with the legal interest added. The workman was thereby relieved of the payment of $15.70 for the use of $50 for thirteen weeks.

The object in giving this illustration is threefold: first, to show that a self-respecting man, who has been independent, will accept any pecuniary obligation imposed on him by a money-lender rather than seek for charitable aid; secondly, to point out that the rate of interest charged by fraudulent loan companies and pawnbrokers is ruinous to the borrower; and, thirdly, to emphasize that the designs of such money-grabbers on the purses of the ignorant borrowers can be thwarted by those that have some legal or business knowledge.

In this country the establishment of pawnshops to lend money at a reasonable rate of interest has been left to private initiative, the

State not establishing, as it has done in so many European countries, public loan shops for the use of its citizens.

The efforts made here by charity workers may be divided into three classes: loans on personal pledges, with or without security, on chattel mortgages, and on pledges of personal effects.

In 1877, Mrs. George S. Jackson of Lexington, Massachusetts, having realized the great need there was of giving the struggling poor of Boston some means of relieving themselves from the clutches of the pawnbrokers, made an appeal to her friends to aid her in establishing a fund for the use of persons that were paying exorbitant rates of interest to money-lenders. She soon appreciated that what the class she wished to reach needed was not to be relieved from a bad bargain, but to be prevented from making a compact with a class of men that showed no mercy in their dealings with unprotected borrowers. She, therefore, established her fund as an Emergency Loan Fund, and, assisted by the Associated Charities, was, and is, able to operate it with but little paid assistance.   For some years no interest was charged on loans, but since 1883 the legal rate of six per cent has been asked.

Each borrower is required to give as security the name of some guarantor.   In the early days of the dispensing of the fund, the effort was made to encourage the borrowers to call on their personal friends to render this service, but latterly it has been found more expedient to have the guarantors drawn from a more moneyed class.   The loans which, as a rule, have been productive of good results are those that have been made to enable the borrower to buy stock, to start in business, or to buy furniture for cash rather than on the instalment plan.   Unsuccessful loans have been those furnished to aid in the payment of back rent.

The experience gained by the treasurer enables her to dispense the loan now with very infrequent losses, and she was able to report in 1894 that out of the last 100 loans, amounting to $4800, all had been, or were being, repaid except four.

In England loan funds established in connection with the district work of the London

Charity Organization Society have been very successful, and have proved that it is possible for such funds to be economically managed and judiciously distributed.

As early as 1855 the Boston Industrial Aid Society for the Prevention of Pauperism urged on the public the need of establishing a "pawnee's bank," so that the poor might be protected from the extortion of the usurious money-lenders.

Five years later the Pawnee's Bank was chartered, and began loaning money with an interest charge of one and one-half per cent a month. In 1867 the Industrial Aid Society reported that the bank[1] did not meet the needs of the class that wished to make small loans.

Mr. Robert Treat Paine realized some years later that the borrower of small sums of money was still at the mercy of the pawnbroker, and that there was urgent need for some institution to be established that could give him cheap credit.

The Workingmen's Loan Association, the

[1] It is now the Collateral Loan Company.

first association of its kind to be organized in
the United States, was opened in Boston in
May, 1888, with a subscribed capital of $66,600.[1]
Its loans are secured by mortgages on furniture
or household effects, and the interest charged
is one per cent a month. All loans are made
repayable in one month, and the renewal of a
loan is dependent on the reliability that has
been evinced by the borrower. He is required
to make an "instalment of the principal equal
to about five per cent of the loan with each
payment of interest," so that the debt may be
gradually cancelled.

Each applicant for a loan, if he satisfac-
torily answer the preliminary questions, is
made to fill out the following form : —

Amount of loan.
Name in full.
What security?
Where is it situated?
Where is your present residence?
How long have you resided there?
Previous residence during the last five years.
What is your business?
Where?

[1] Capital stock now issued amounts to $150,000.

Have you receipted bills for the property?
Does all the property belong to you?
Is there any incumbrance on it?
Name two references.
What amount of principal will you pay monthly?
Do you agree to pay interest promptly?
Is your property insured, and for how much?

After the form has been filled in and the would-be borrower has made a deposit of 35 cents, an appraiser calls at the residence of the former to make a careful estimate of the value of the property that is to be given as security. The borrower is allowed a loan equal to three-fourths of the amount that the appraiser calculates the property would bring at an auction sale. When satisfactory evidence is given that the property is unencumbered, the amount of the loan less the costs (amounting to $1.65, minus the 35 cents already paid) is handed to the applicant.

On all sums over $100 the borrower has to give to the association an insurance policy, made payable to it for the goods mortgaged; for a loan of less than this amount a deposit of $1 or 50 cents, according to the size of the loan, is required as an insurance guarantee. In case of a sale of mortgaged property, any surplus that the company may hold, after the sum secured by the mortgage, the costs, and the counsel fees have been deducted, is returned to the mortgagee.

The company has been able to declare dividends of two per cent the first year, four per cent the second, and six per cent each subsequent year, and has at present a guaranty fund of $15,332.19. The number of borrowers is now 2438, an increase of 287 during the past year. The loans made during the year amounted to $151,660.90, or an average loan of $70. The last fiscal year, after charging $659.46 for bad debts, paying six per cent dividends on stock, and meeting all the expenses and charges, a surplus of $5054.48 remained.

The policy of the association has been to avoid lending more than is needed to meet the emergency that calls forth the loan, and to make the borrower feel that he is dealing with a business enterprise.

In New York City the St. Bartholomew's Loan Association has proved that it is feasible

for a church to undertake to conduct such a
business without establishing it on a charitable
basis. Any church organization can with a
small capital open a loan bureau. It must
never be lost sight of, however, that such a
bureau must be managed by competent business men or women, and must be in no way
connected with any church charity.

In 1895 a law was passed in New York
which made it legal for provident loan companies to be organized in the state. Under
the provisions of this law was organized the
Buffalo Provident Loan Company, which has
conducted a business very similar to that of
the Workingmen's Loan Association.

As early as 1877 the State Charities Aid
Association of New York appointed a committee to make a report on loan systems. The
report urged the formation of loan associations
as auxiliaries to existing societies, and as an
outcome a loan relief association was founded
the next year. This association was organized
on the principle of relief in work, with payments in advance for work to be done. Other
loan societies were organized, but it was not

until seventeen years later that a provident
loan association on a large scale was established. In 1894 the Provident Loan Society
of New York, the direct result of the zealous
efforts of the Charity Organization Society,
was organized with a contributed capital of
$100,000. The demands on the society were so
great that in a few months the whole amount
of the capital was outstanding in loans, and
the treasurer had to be authorized to borrow
additional moneys to the amount of $40,000.

All loans are made on pledges of jewellery
or clothes deposited at the office. The class
of borrowers has been drawn from the self-
respecting working men and women, who are
not willing to ask for charitable aid. The interest on loans is one per cent a month. As
with the Workingmen's Loan Association any
surplus that remains to the company after the
pledged articles are sold is returned to the
borrower.

In 1897 $764,926.50 was loaned on 36,772
pledges, or an average loan of $20.80. The
shareholders received six per cent interest on
their stock, and, after all expenses were met,

about $15,000 was accredited to the reserve
fund. The percentage of goods sold in 1897
to the total amount loaned was less than two
per cent.

One of the important effects of the establishment of provident loan societies has been
that in each city in which they have been organized the pawnbrokers have tried to protect
themselves by lowering their rates of interest.
The pawnbrokers so clearly realize the danger
that threatens them in the establishment of
such agencies, that they have in different
states successfully fought the passing of laws
to legalize provident loan companies based on
a charter such as that of the Workingmen's
Loan Association or the New York Provident
Loan·Society.

It has been proved that if a loan is to be
successful it must be controlled by an organization rather than by an individual, and that
the borrower must be made clearly to realize
that he is dealing with a business enterprise.
The story is told of a workman who had joined
a benefit society and was regularly paying his
dues, though he had failed to repay his vicar

the sum of money he had borrowed from him. One day the vicar asked his man for an explanation of his inconsistency, and the only answer he got was: "Ah, you're the vicar, you don't want it." The workman appreciated that there is a difference between the relations of a rich man to a poor man and between the members of a mutual benefit association. Was it his fault that his recognition of the obligation imposed by a loan had become dimmed?

The repayment of each loan must be secured by some guarantee, either a surety or a mortgage on household or personal effects. In spite of Mrs. Jackson's experience, the guarantor should be chosen from the same rank of life as the borrower, because the latter should never be tempted to say to his surety, "You don't want it," but should be made to feel that it is a friend, and one that has borne the brunt of the battle for existence, who has to make good his failure to repay his debt.[1]

[1] The treasurer of an English loan fund has reported that out of more than a thousand applications he has never known a case in which a deserving person failed to find a surety among his acquaintances, if his neighbors felt the loan to be expedient.

In making a loan it should be considered whether the money lent is sufficient to meet the demand that has called it forth, and whether the purpose to which it is put is one that is going to yield any return. Here again it is necessary to bear in mind that money lent to "stop a hole" is money put to no productive purpose. The past habits of the borrower, the use of the loan, and the practical ability of the borrower should all be taken into account in considering an application.

It is also necessary to bear in mind that a loan system is intended to supersede alms-giving, not to "supplement or precede it," and that no loan should be made in cases where it is clear that the borrower will be unable to make good his debt. Such an applicant should be referred to the proper charitable agency, for a loan under such conditions would mean a mere staving off a day of reckoning.

In arranging for the payment of interest on a loan, it is well to name a day that will fall soon after the borrower has received his regular wages. It is most important, also, that the loans should be repaid in instalments, not only because the debt will fall less heavily, but because the educational effect of putting by weekly a regular sum may develop the habit of saving, and lead, as it has in many instances, to depositing, after the loan is repaid, in a savings bank. There should not be, however, cast-iron rules, for in the case of some loans it may be detrimental to the borrower to be required to make any repayment until his money has had time to reproduce itself.

The fundamental principle of these associations, such as have been described, is that they should help without "degrading or enervating." It is, therefore, necessary that any promoter of such societies should realize that there has been imposed on him a trust that he should never violate, and that in violating this trust he is wronging a self-respecting class, which is trying to meet the obligations imposed on it. No spirit of helpfulness, no sentiment for the poor or effort to reach the class of the unthrifty, is an excuse for those who would offer to the workingman a loan as a business arrangement, when beneath a veneer of business methods lies a foundation of charitable aid.

In reviewing the work of the people's banks and that of these associations, we can but feel that in the former there is developed a power to watch the loan which cannot be superimposed on the provident loan associations. The latter are doing good service, but can never meet the needs of the working classes as do the mutual associations. In a mutual loan association, where each member is scrutinizing the moral and economic behavior of his fellows, there is no need for a high rate of interest to be charged in the fear that borrowing will be encouraged.

It is not intended to minimize the good that has been done by these associations, which have realized that the poor have to meet a call for ready money, and that they must be rescued from a class of extortioners; but it is hoped that when it is feasible the higher forms of borrowing will be encouraged.

L

CHAPTER VII

INSURANCE

THERE are certain demands made by nature, which can only be met if men will in seasons of health make adequate provision for the periods of enforced inactivity. Only in as far as each man realizes his individual responsibility, by laying by for a time of sickness or disability, can he remain through life independent and avoid the stigma of pauper or parasite. The act of making provision in youth or middle age for disability or for death necessitates that a man should exercise foresight and self-control, as well as self-denial. But he who by means of insurance has made "the claims of the future take definite shape and rank among the claims of the present," has advanced far beyond his fellow that lives merely in the present and for the present. The latter will have to learn, like the grass-

hopper in the fable, that one cannot dance all
the summer without being obliged to go hungry
from door to door, when the frugal ant who
has "provided her meat in the summer and
gathered her food in the harvest" is enjoying
the fruits of her hard labor.

In America, the principal form of saving
is life insurance, and it is natural that such
should be the case in a country where the
resources of nature have seemed to offer to
every man opportunities that might at any
time open to him a vein of wealth. As, however, even the most sanguine knows that he
has to provide against the universal accident
of death, an effort has been made by many
to insure against death, when no attempt has
been made to save for a time of non-employment or of sickness.

We have not yet been confronted with the
question of compulsory insurance against sickness, accident, and old age and disability.
The "tradition, historical continuity, a strongly
centralized bureaucracy," [1] which have made it

---

[1] *American Journal of Sociology*, "An American System of
Labor Pensions and Insurance," Vol. II., p. 501.

consistent for the Germans, a people accustomed to await the collective initiative, to legislate to make insurance compulsory, are wanting to us, so that there is in the United States no room for such a class system, the establishment of which would be· "preposterous." Our insurance agencies for many years to come must be established on a purely commercial basis, if they are to meet the requirements of the people.

In 1891, Mr. Carroll D. Wright, the United States Commissioner of Labor, considered the subject of compulsory insurance of sufficient importance to warrant an expert's being engaged to make a special report on the subject. Mr. John Graham Brooks was, therefore, empowered to make such a report.[1]

Mr. Brooks shows that the passing of the laws to make it compulsory for certain classes of workingmen to insure their lives against sickness, accident, and old age, was the result of socialistic activity, and the recognition of the fact that certain misfortunes are often

[1] Fourth Special Report of the Commissioner of Labor, "Compulsory Insurance in Germany," etc., 1893.

produced by social conditions rather than by individual carelessness or lack of forethought. Also, that before compulsory insurance was enforced in Germany, it had long been held as an "economic theory" by many thinkers, that a natural step in the economic and political policy of Prussia would be for the State to make the financially weak provide for their future by levying a tax on their wages, the sum so accumulated to be augmented by the State and the employers.

In 1883 the act was passed that made it compulsory for nearly all classes of working-men, earning less than $476 per annum, to lay aside a part of their wages for a sick and death benefit. Though premiums may be taken in any one of several insurance associations — such as the communal, the building, and the friendly society, — the tendency has been to centralize the insurance agencies, and so to destroy the mutual societies. As each workman has his contribution deducted from his wages, there is no difficulty in collecting the premiums, which amount to from one per cent to four and one-half per cent of his wages.

The workman contributes two-thirds of the premium, the employer the remaining one-third. In ten years $180,166,000 has been paid to workingmen on account of sickness.[1]

The law making it compulsory for employers to insure the lives of their employees against accident was passed in 1884; and during the past ten years, $45,934,000[2] has been paid to workingmen suffering from accidents, or to their families in case of their death.

In 1889 the law making insurance against old age and disability compulsory was passed. According to this law, a pension may be drawn by a man aged seventy, who for thirty years has made regular contributions to the pension fund, and by a disabled man, who for five years has paid his premiums. The expense of this insurance is borne by the State, the employer, and the employee. Pensions have been paid to 101,544 chronic invalids,[3] and to 241,700 aged persons.[4] The total sum paid

---

[1] Report, Consul Monaghan, Chemnitz, Germany.

[2] *Ibid.*   [3] *Ibid.*

[4] The reason for granting the old age pensions at once has been in order to popularize the system.

out in ten years has been $238,000,000, forty-seven and one-half per cent of which has been paid by the employers.

In 1896, 18,389,000 persons were insured in Germany under this system, and of this number, 3,409,000 were employees in factories or shops, 12,290,000 were agricultural laborers, and 690,000 were employees of the State.

Mr. Brooks says that in 1893 the first insurance act was in wide favor, the second in favor, and the third disliked by a large and influential part of the population.

In spite of the development of the German bureaucracy, the State has to incur, in addition to its bounty, an enormous expense so as to enforce the system of insurance, and collect the premiums and distribute the policies.

The results of the German system will be watched with deep interest, and to the economist and the sociologist will be left the decision as to whether the burden of the enforced contributions falls on the consumer, the workingman, or the employer; whether the system develops or kills the spirit of self-help; and whether the alarming tendency to play sick, when work is scarce or rent day comes, can be overcome by more rigid physical examinations.

Germany has served as an object-lesson to Austria, Switzerland, France, Denmark, and other European countries, which have been experimenting· in different ways, either by voluntary or compulsory insurance, with the problem of providing for the working classes in times of sickness and disability. For many years Great Britain has offered to her people a system of voluntary insurance against old age and death, but the limited success of the post-office life insurance and old age pensions has made such reformers and politicians as Mr. Charles Booth and Mr. Chamberlain demand a compulsory system, which will give a sure footing to those who are on the "brink of pauperism." Though such writers as Mr. Leslie Stephen think that indiscriminate giving of State relief would "ruin the essential economic virtues," and other prominent English students of social questions are ready to declare that a State-aided pension would put a premium on thriftlessness, and that thrift on compulsion is no thrift at all, there are those who believe with Mr. Booth that the small pension received by a man at sixty-five years of age will encourage thrift (since he that has wants more), and will strengthen rather than enervate existing benefit societies.

The advocates of the system, many of whom are men that for years have been earnest and conscientious students of the great problems of our social life, see the mass of old age pauperism, and feel that it is only by State intervention that any adequate provision can be made for the care in old age of the self-respecting poor. Though many disagree with Mr. Booth, because they believe his reasoning is fallacious, all will be ready to say with him, "that any pension scheme would be fatal if it in any way disturbed the basis of work and wages, discouraged thrift, or undermined, even in the slightest degree, self-respect or the forces of individuality, upon which morality as well as industry depends."

May there be no legislation in England to make insurance compulsory until a sufficient test of the experiment in Germany has made it possible for other nations to determine whether, under different conditions and with different peoples, such a system is opposed to the highest development of a nation.

Opposed to the voluntary or compulsory system of State insurance is the commercial, which by its industrial policies has reached such a vast number of people both in this country and in England. Like all other savings agencies, the insurance companies have been obliged to adapt themselves to the "needs and humors" of their customers. Their adaptability has been shown by the way in which they have appreciated that what the poor want is to be saved the trouble and the expenditure of time which are required if a savings depository has to be sought. Their shrewdness they have shown by their manner of playing on one of the most ingrained characteristics of the poor — their respect for the dead.

In one of Robert Morrison's "Tales of Mean Streets," a dreadful picture is shown of an old woman that deprives her dying son of the stimulants the doctor has given her the money to buy for him, so that he may be decently buried. To her neighbor "On the Stairs" she croaks in the "full morning" after her son has died: —

"I'm a-goin' to 'ave mutes; I can do it respectable, thank Gawd."

"And the plumes?" queries her gaunt friend.

"Ah, yes, and the ploomes, too."

Though this shows the worst development of the sentiment that the poor have for their dead, and suggests that the desire for a decent burial may degenerate into a mere selfish gratification of conventional traditions, in dealing with the poor it has to be remembered that each class of people has its social laws, and that each individual who helps to make a group must bear an intrinsic relation to the group as a whole. Even in the meanest streets society exercises a dominant force on each inhabitant, and an attempt to attack thoughtlessly any of the traditions of a neighborhood can but end in failure.

The charity worker is constantly met by the problem, how to enlighten the poor on the subject of burials, and how to teach them that

industrial life insurance is a very expensive
form of saving, and that a man should provide against the misfortunes of sickness, slack-
ness of work, and old age before he provides
for funeral benefits; but he is as constantly
met by the deep-rooted sentiment that it is a
degradation to let the city bury one's dead,
and that to allow the city to perform such
an act would mean that a family deserved to
become social outcasts.

As has been said, therefore, the industrial
insurance companies have shown their wisdom
in appealing to this sentiment of the poor for
their dead, but they have shown greater wisdom in opening an agency in the house of
every poor man that will make use of it, and
in returning week after week to collect the
hard-won savings. An official of one of the
most successful of the industrial insurance
companies says it does not differ from ordinary insurance except that it enables the poor
man to pay a premium as low as five cents
for his policy, and that an agent calls weekly
to collect it.

The success of the system depends on the

number that are insured in each family, so it
is an agent's policy to insure all the members
of a household, "to take them from two to
seventy years of age," and the agent is sure
to be a special pleader and to be ready to go
any lengths to collect the nickels and the dimes,
for his own commission is entirely dependent
on the number of premiums he is able to
collect and on the preventing of lapsing.

In England, during the last half century,
mutual thrift is said to have flowed into two
main channels, that of the affiliated orders,
and of the collecting burial societies. The
latter class has lost, however, its mutual character, for the benefits go to the managers, the
meetings are seldom attended by the members, and the cost to the insured for management is forty per cent of the premium receipts.
Early in the fifties, a committee of Parliament
was appointed to study the methods and the
results of the assurance associations. In its
report in 1853, the committee said that its
opinion was, "that the ground hitherto occu-
pied by these useful institutions (assurance
associations) has been comparatively limited,

and that their application is capable of great extension, not only in the higher and middle classes of society, but also among the humble classes to which it has recently been very considerably applied." The directors of one of the proprietary assurance companies had their attention called to the above sentence, and they decided in 1854 to begin business on the industrial plan so as to compete with the burial clubs, which were in a precarious condition. This great pioneer of the strictly commercial system of industrial life insurance is managed with very great ability, and has a practically perfect system of audit. The cost of management for the industrial branch is 41.47 per cent of the premium income, but " as a very large number of ordinary insurances are now being taken up in connection with it, what used to be the main business, industrial insurance, has now become quite a minor feature of its programme." As the insured transfers his policy from the more to the less expensive form, he is saved a large outlay. The management of the average ordinary assurance company in England costs 16.4 per cent of the receipts, the industrial 44.36 per cent.

In 1876 one of the insurance companies of America began to do business on an industrial plan identical with that of the London company. At the end of its first year, twenty-five hundred industrial policies were in force. The appended table[1] shows the rapid progress of the industrial insurance movement.

	No. of Companies	No. of pol. in force	Insurance in force
1876	1	2,500	$ 248,342
1880	3	228,357	19,590,780
1885	3	1,360,376	144,101,632
1890	9	3,875,102	428,037,245
1897	10	7,985,352	994,197,057[2]

In this country great opposition to industrial insurance has been made on the ground, that the insuring of the lives of children is a temptation to the parents either directly to murder their offspring, or indirectly to cause their death by giving them insufficient food.

[1] The "Spectator Insurance Year Book," 1898, p. 251.
[2] The average policy being, therefore, for $124.

This accusation has led to the effort that has been made by individuals and by societies to prevent the insuring of the lives of children under ten or twelve years of age. ·The different bills that have been introduced into various state legislatures have failed, just as similar efforts have in Canada and England, not only because the companies have made a strong fight for their privileges, but because the public has realized that, as an English physician, who has had experience in examining candidates for industrial insurance policies, writes: "It would be as rational to interdict fire insurance, because of a few cases of arson, as to prohibit child insurance because of a few cases of infanticide." As the average policy for a child is $28, it can hardly be looked on as a great inducement to murder, when, in order to procure payment, the beneficiary will have to submit himself to a rigid examination by the company, which is most anxious to protect its own position.

As the companies do not insure the lives of children under one year of age, they only begin to grant. death benefits after the age of greatest mortality is passed. The experience of the companies is that their death rate is lower than that of the general population, and they give as their reason, that insurance tends to raise the standard of living by teaching thrift and economy.[1] Though the lower death rate is a refutation of the charge that infantile insurance brings about child neglect, it also shows that the insurance companies do not go into the worst quarters of a city, and that they, therefore, avoid taking the risk of insuring that class of the population that is subject to the highest death rate.

The limit of the premium payable by a child under ten years of age is, in the largest of the industrial life insurance companies, ten cents per week,[2] and the duplication of child insurance is prohibited.

---

[1] A college settlement worker of great experience writes: "I am sure all the settlement people I know would say that industrial insurance is specious and unreliable as a method of saving and without relation to thrift. So far as such insurance is collected, it goes in the main to undertakers and is swallowed up in the pomp of a funeral."

[2] In order to get a knowledge of the cost of industrial insurance, the reader is referred to the Appendix, Table I.

M

The companies do strive to prevent speculation in child insurance on the part of parents
or guardians. If, however, the tables be criti-
cally examined, it can but be realized that, in
proportion to the amount of the policies, the
premiums are ruinously large. Yet the companies claim that a policy must have run into
the third year before, as an official of one of
the large companies says, "we make money,
and every policy that lapses before that time,
is a loss to us. . . . We have to collect two
years to pay initial expenses."

The experience of the companies has been,
as has been that of the charity worker, that the
money paid for children's policies is "considered sacred to be used to meet funeral expenses," and that to devote this money to any
other use is looked on as "a robbing of the
dead."

In Orange, New Jersey, a successful insurance collector went into the undertaking business, so clearly did he realize that the holders
of life insurance policies would be able to
meet the expenses of the funerals. Though
the money is not directly payable to an under-

taker (the sound companies having refused to coöperate in any way with physicians or undertakers), he knows that in twenty-four hours after a death the policy will be paid, and that he can certainly collect his bill, which is often gauged by what he knows to be the value of the policy.

December 31, 1897, the three large industrial life insurance companies had 1,566,765 children under ten years of age insured. The experience of the companies is that the infantile class is the most persistent, the number of lapses being, therefore, in it more infrequent than in the adult. To the child policy issued for the whole of life no reserve feature has to be attached by ˙the companies, as the risk is considered to be carried by the year and no paid up policies are due or dividends declarable until the child enters the adult class.[1]

The cost of management has been already mentioned, and to give a concrete example of the relative cost of management to policies paid, the following table is appended: —

[1] Adult class begins at age ten.

1897

METROPOLITAN:	Total payments to policy holders	$7,329,908.61 [1]
	Expense	8,659,362.98 [2]
	Total disbursements .	$15,989,271.59
PRUDENTIAL:	Total payments, etc. .	$4,522,931.74 [1]
	Expense	5,743,438.44
	Total disbursements .	$10,266,370.18
JOHN HANCOCK:	Total payments, etc. .	$1,594,076.00 [1]
	Expenses	1,991,736.00
	Total disbursements .	$3,585,812.00

It is very easy to realize how great is the cost of the mere machinery of these companies, when we appreciate that there are tens of thousands of agents in the field, that they have in the home offices thousands of clerks to carry on the business of correspondence and to transmit death claims, and that in order to protect the business three grades of agents have to be put in charge of the district work. They are a superintendent, that has executive charge of a district, who receives in addition to a salary a contingent interest paid "on the basis of an increase in the business," an assist-

[1] Excludes the ordinary life insurance of the company.
[2] For analysis, see Appendix, Table III.

ant superintendent, who has charge of six or eight agents for whose fidelity to their trust he is responsible, and a body of agents that combine the three functions of 'canvassers, solicitors, and collectors. The last receive fifteen per cent of all premiums collected and a commission for increase of business, but each is obliged to make good a lapsed policy before he can receive his commission, the agents thus sharing with the company the loss from lapsing.

The incentive to make large collections being so strong, it is not strange that the average pay of an agent in a city should be between ten and eleven dollars a week, and that he should see to it that the whole family, from the baby to the grandfather, is insured.

In spite of the great effort that is made by the companies to prevent lapsing, the following table shows how small has been their success:—

1897

METROPOLITAN:	No. of policies issued	. .	1,398,899
	" " " terminated	.	1,013,646
PRUDENTIAL:	" " " issued	. .	1,008,868
	" " " terminated	.	747,074 .
JOHN HANCOCK:	" " " issued	. .	269,522
	" " " terminated	.	205,455

A prominent life insurance company stated before the Massachusetts legislature in 1895 that during the first year of writing fifty-two per cent of the policies lapse, during the second year, thirteen per cent, and during the third, four per cent. This includes the death claims, policies discontinued by a return of the premiums, and those surrendered for paid-up policies.

Another one of the companies tries to prevent lapsing by carefully guarding the standard of admission, but, in spite of its efforts, the percentage of terminated policies is ninety. In 1880, it issued 524,915 policies; of these, fifty per cent lapsed during the first year, sixteen per cent the second, five per cent the third, three per cent the fourth, and two per cent each subsequent year. To prevent premature lapsing an agent is allowed to keep an unpaid policy on his books for four weeks, so that the insured may have an opportunity of making good his arrears.

As the lapse rate is greatest in the first three months of writing, the loss to the lapsed policy holder is small, and against this pecuniary loss must be put the protection that has been granted during the weeks in which the policy was in force. The very fact, however, that the premium payments are discontinued shows that the class which is insured either lacks the available means to become policy holders or are too thriftless to persist in saving. In either case the investment has been demoralizing to the intermittent saver. It has withdrawn from immediate consumption a much needed part of the weekly wage, or, because unpersisted in, has reacted unfavorably on the quondam policy holder.

The solvency of the three largest industrial companies in 1896 was shown by the "Insurance Year Book," which stated that they had a surplus of $9,745,927, the assets being $58,995,508, the liabilities, $49,249,581.

The grip that industrial insurance has taken can best be shown by giving the city of Newark, New Jersey, as an example. In that city, a population of 231,000 hold in the three large companies 222,013 policies. According to a census of policy holders above the age of ten, taken by one of the companies in 1896, the number of women insured was 1,032,908, of men, 1,023,509. Of the former class,

568,515 were engaged in household work, 97,015 were domestic servants, and 123,965 were factory operatives; of the latter class, 181,164 were outdoor laborers, 83,266 indoor laborers, 123,597 factory operatives, and 142,415 were mechanics.

The industrial insurance companies have a great advantage over other commercial enterprises in that they are not called on to advertise their business, except by making liberal offers to their policy holders. They do try to prevent lapsing by issuing a bi-monthly paper and by circulating pamphlets, which show the insured how much to his advantage it is to continue to carry his policy, but the only systematic form of advertisement they need is an occasional death, especially of a child.

It can be said that the industrial companies cannot, on account of the risks they run, and the great expense they have to incur in collecting the small weekly sums, charge a much less high premium.[1]   The risks are greater

[1] In the words of one of the insurance officers, "If the premiums were reduced one cent a week it would lead to insolvency."

than in the ordinary companies, because, as the industrial companies cannot afford to pay a doctor's fee for a careful examination, the insurance is not based on a high selection of lives. A physician does, however, inspect each applicant and act as a check to the cupidity of the agent. The death rate is lower this year than during past years, being 34.22 per cent of the premiums collected, which proves (the law of averages determining that the ratio of deaths in the general population in any given year will be equal to that of any other year) that more care is being taken in inspecting the applicants.

The advantages of the industrial form of insurance may be summed up in the words of a fair critic of the work of the London Prudential, who, in a private letter to the author, says: "It is certain that the money would not be secured for any thrift purpose in the population with which the Prudential is largely concerned, except by house to house visitation. To me the society appears to be a wonderful instance of the success which attends those who choose to work upon some instinctive want on the part of a people, and elaborate their system first in connection with it, and then in connection with higher wants, which people by degrees desire to satisfy."

It may be said in addition that the death benefit has lessened the number of pauper funerals, and, thereby, has made a large body of the poorer class independent of a demoralizing form of poor relief.

In the report of the "Select Committee of the House of Commons on Collecting Friendly Societies, and Industrial Assurance Companies," for 1889, it was said, "The Committee are compelled to look upon the methods of collecting societies as of no value whatever towards education in thrift." Without going as far as this report, it can but be realized that industrial insurance is the most elementary form of provident saving, and a friendly visitor can do no better work than to try to divert the savings of the poor into less expensive channels and urge them to "forego the costly luxury of collecting insurance."

It is well to show that money invested in a life insurance policy is withdrawn from any immediately productive use, and that there is need first to provide for the claims that are not posthumous by insuring against sickness, non-employment, and old age. There is nothing beautiful about an almshouse pauper who can draw out an insurance book taken in better days, and say, "I won't have to be buried by the city," nor about a family which receives outdoor relief, either from the city or from private sources, while it is meeting the weekly demands of the collector.

What the charity worker must clearly realize is, that "a real family insurance," the "two to seventy years of age," is an absurdity. In the code of instructions to physicians mentioned before, an insurable interest is defined as being one where the "death of the insured is a pecuniary loss to the beneficiary." It can hardly be questioned that it is a poor speculation to insure the lives of children who have not reached the age of productivity or old people who have passed that bourne. Children *do* die and families *are* greatly benefited by receiving a paid-in policy when the purse holds no surplus to meet the funeral charges; but these patent facts should not be considered as an argument for infantile insurance. The only member of a family that should, from an economic standpoint, be insured, is he or she who is the provider of the support of the family.

A danger that has to be guarded against is the fraud that may be committed by unscrupulous collectors who are ready to cheat the poor by extravagant estimates of the value of an insurance policy, and an evil is that the poor are led by the holding of an insurance policy to indulge in extravagant funerals.

But in spite of the great expense that industrial insurance entails on the poor, the danger of fraudulent collectors getting their money because of false assertions, and the evils that may arise from encouraging extravagance in burials, it can but be repeated that no general crusade, no legislative enactment, can undermine a system that is based on a strongly developed sentiment.

In an earlier chapter it has been shown that a temporary expedient is to have the stamp savings system go to the people, but the present chapter proves that such an effort can only be limited in scope and temporary in character. Any general system of collecting would be subject to the same criticism as the industrial insurance companies, namely, that it is too expensive to be borne by the poor.

What can and should be done is, whenever and wherever it is possible, to make the poor appreciate what they are paying for their insurance policies, and urge them to divert their premiums from industrial to ordinary branches. Publicity should be given to the distinction between ordinary and industrial insurance, so that the poor may not be kept in ignorance of the greater advantage that is being offered by the latter.

In the Appendix is a Table[1] that shows the cost of a $500 policy in the intermediate branch of one of the large industrial life insurance companies. As premiums are payable to a collector, quarterly, semi-annually, or annually, instead of weekly, the cost of management is very much smaller and the chances of lapsing

[1] Table IV.

are much fewer than in the industrial branch.
The intermediate branch is intended to serve
as a bridge between the industrial and the old
line companies, and to reach the better class
of mechanics and laborers.

To show the hold that industrial insurance
has in the United States the following table
is appended:—

1895

Policy holders in Industrial Life Ins. Cos. . . 6,944,000
    "   "   " Ordinary " " " . . 1,877,808 [1]
Depositors in Savings Banks 4,975,519

The forms of insurance, apart from industrial
life insurance, are so numerous, and the companies and associations organized to grant insurance so many and so diverse in character,
that it is not possible even to mention more
than a few. The kinds of risks on which a
policy may be taken cover the whole field of
industry, from credit insurance, organized to
insure merchants against loss from giving credit
to their customers, to the French peasant system of insuring against loss by unavoidable

[1] Companies reporting to the New York Insurance Department.

failure in the crops.[1] What must be alluded to, however, are insurance against sickness and accident. Their importance is so great that the following chapter will treat of what the English friendly societies are doing to meet the need of the workingman to guard against the loss of independence on account of sickness or chronic disability. Unfortunately space is so limited that mention only can be made of what trades unions, railway companies, and workingmen's clubs are doing to offer their members the "expedient of insurance."

Though the benevolent features of the trades unions are said to be still in an experimental state,[2] nearly all the unions have funds for members in distress. In addition to death benefits, varying from $40 to $550, sick relief is given in weekly sums varying from $3 to $5, and hospital beds are maintained in large cities for the use of members. In Colorado is a home for sick, disabled, old, and infirm members of the International Typographical Union. Some

[1] See Chap. IV. p. 97, and VI. p. 137.
[2] John D. Flanigan, ex-president of the Michigan Federation of Labor.

unions have established funds for the relief of members out of work, and to pay the travelling expenses of those who are in search of employment.

In addition to the relief offered by such organizations of employees as the International Brotherhood of Locomotive Engineers, the Brotherhood of Railroad Trainmen, and the Order of Railway Conductors, the employees of six great railroad systems may under compulsion or voluntarily become members of their relief departments. The funds, which are partly contributed by the railroads and partly by the employees, are used to give systematic and comprehensive relief covering sickness, accident, old age, and death.

The first railroad in the United States to establish a relief department was the Baltimore and Ohio, which in 1880 organized its Employees' Relief Association. In 1888 the Association was dissolved, and in less than a year the present relief department was formed, membership in which is compulsory on all employees of the road who receive less than $2000 a year or more than $20 a month. The department is divided into three sections: the relief, the savings, and the pension. The first gives relief in times of sickness and of death; the second offers to members and their near relatives a safe place of deposit, and, to the former only, a fund from which to borrow in order to acquire a homestead, or to improve it, or free it from debt; the last assures a competence to the aged and infirm who are retired or relieved by the road.

In 1886 the Pennsylvania Railroad organized its relief department, membership in which is voluntary. The cost of life insurance to members is about the same as in the orders and the brotherhoods, but is less than in the ordinary or old line companies. The cost of accident and sick benefits is less than in either the brotherhood or the stock companies.[1]

Objections have been brought by labor organizations against these departments because they are said to retard the growth of labor organizations and to protect the companies against

[1] "Railway Departments for the Relief and Insurance of Employees," by E. R. Johnson, American Academy Political and Social Science, pp. 103-105.

N

suits for damages.   In reply it is stated that they guarantee better service, and so protect the travelling public, and that each member is free either to accept a benefit or to sue the company.

Mr. O. D. Ashley[1] approves of relief departments' being entirely controlled by the employers, the employees not being asked to contribute directly to the funds.   Such a system would, however, destroy the mutual feature of such associations.

It is not railroads alone that have tried to solve the grave problem of how to make the interests of employer and employee identical by organizing relief departments for their men.   Apart from the profit sharing schemes, many employers of labor have established relief associations.

In connection with the Wells Memorial Institute of Boston is a benefit association for the use of the male members.   In 1898, at the end of the tenth year of its organization, it had eighty members.   At the end of each year, the membership terminates and each member receives his proportion of the surplus that remains in the treasury.   In 1896–1897 the dues

[1] " Railways and their Employees," p. 54.

and fees amounted to $455.55, sick benefits to
$85, and death benefits to $50. Each member had returned to him $4.14, or nearly two-
thirds of what he had contributed. On the
back of the circular that advertised the association, was printed: "Can you improve on
this plan in any other organization within
your knowledge?" Without accepting this
challenge, it may be remarked that such a
sharing out club "cannot be regarded as a
serious way of providing for the risks of the
future." A serious objection is that a man
who falls into ill health may be precluded
from membership at the time when he most
needs his club, and another objection is that
there is no guarantee that a constant membership will be maintained.

There can be no educational value in such
an association apart from that which is got
in making the regular monthly contributions.

Similar organizations may be found in many
churches and clubs, but it is to be regretted
that no further illustration can be drawn. No
adequate idea can, unfortunately, be given of
the number and the character of the associa-

tions that are providing death benefits for their members. In workingmen and working-girls' clubs, in churches, educational institutes, fraternal societies, and unions of all kinds may be found benefit features; from the simplest form, a mere demand on the general treasury for the discharge of a sick benefit, to the most complex. Whatever may be the form, however, the association using it should provide against insolvency by basing the calculation as to what the dues should be on some sound actuarial system.

To the charity worker who is able to persuade another to provide for the demands of the incalculable future, will come the gratification of knowing that there is one more who need not fear an "atropos of his fortunes before that of his life." [1]

---

[1] Recently an effort has been made in Chicago, by a business firm, to provide insurance against non-employment. The difficulties, however, in the way of the success of such a plan are so great (as has been proved in St. Gall, Switzerland, where compulsory insurance against non-employment was enforced for a short period of time), and the business arrangements are as yet so tentative, that it cannot be described here, valuable as insurance against non-employment would be if it were practicable. See *American Journal of Sociology*, May, 1897, Vol. II. p. 771.

CHAPTER VIII

ENGLISH FRIENDLY SOCIETIES

IT is not possible in a few words to describe the great friendly society movement so as to give a just conception of what the societies have sprung from or of what they have accomplished, nor does the limited space permit any parallel between the English societies and the American fraternals. It is to be hoped, however, that what is here left undone may be done by some one interested in the general welfare of the workingman, and that it may not be long before the charity worker will have in his library a book that will fully treat of the present status and of the prospective standing of the fraternal societies in this country.

The object in choosing two of the most prominent English societies is to give some general idea of what are the principles that should guide any body of men in providing for themselves a common fund from which to draw an effectual provision in time of sickness or of death.

The friendly societies have been said to be first in the "thrift race" of those organizations which are coöperative in form, and to be "noble institutions of self-help which the working classes of England have made for themselves without any assistance from the government or from the rich."[1]

There are now thirteen societies in England that were established before the middle of the eighteenth century and more than one hundred, in England and Scotland, that were organized before the year 1800. As early as 1797 the great importance of these societies was recognized by Sir F. Eden, who, in his book on the "State of the Poor," says: "That these institutions (friendly societies) increase the comforts of the laboring classes who belong to them will be evident from comparing the conditions of those who are members of them, and of those who in the same village are contented to rely on the parish for relief. The

[1] T. Mackay.

former are generally comparatively cleanly, orderly, and sober, and consequently happy and good members of society ; whilst the latter are living in filth and wretchedness, and are often, from the pressure of casual sickness or accident, which incapacitates them from work-ing, tempted to the commission of improper acts (not to say crimes), against which the sure resource of a benefit club would have been the best preservative."

In the early days, the societies had an elab-orate ritual, and new members were made to take most solemn "oaths and obligations" and to wear symbolic dress. Extracts from an old cash book of the Ancient Oddfellows show the expenses of the lodge for the first year of its existence : —

	£	s.	d.
By Cash-Dispensation . . .	10	10	0
Spirits of Mizalto	1	13	5½
Alfried the Great	2	15	4
For making the Gowns . . .	0	10	0
Six Beards	0	12	6
Hail Storm	0	8	6
Copper Spoon	0	1	0
Silk for Scarfs	20	0	0
Sun and Moon	0	16	0

The silk was bought to be sold at retail to the members, the spirit to be burned in the copper spoon, and the hail-storm for use in the tempest scene.   Alfred the Great was and is the name of a cognate society to which the then new lodge was indebted to the sum of £2 15s. 4d.

Politics played a part in the young days of the friendlies, and we find that one lodge had to close its doors because of the indiscretion of two of its members — the notorious Wilkes and Sir George Saville — in denouncing the government at a lodge meeting.   For many years the friendly societies had to contend against "parliamentary interference" and also against the demoralizing effect of poor law relief.   But in spite of State interference the larger societies remained true to their high ideal of being a real brotherhood, and tentatively worked out their " un-state-aided " economic salvation. They remained mutual societies independent of outside assistance, and, as a rule, guarded their conduct lest they should, as Robert Owen said, injure the institution to which they belonged.   They stood, at a time when the contagion of indiscriminate public relief was killing the self-respect of the laborer, for "the absolute independence" of the working classes, and they proved, as Sir F. Eden showed, that, in spite of poor wages and hard times, forethought and frugality can enable a body of men to organize provident institutions that will yield a subsistence in times of sickness, a subsistence that will make the members independent of the workhouse and of the parish.

But it must not be supposed that the friendly society movement was uninfluenced by the subtle workings of the poor law system. Numbers of men, who were capable of providing for the casualties of life, were prevented by the feeling that they belonged already to a benefit club in which there is "no paying in " and all "paying out." One meeting, which was called for the purpose of forming a new lodge, was adjourned indefinitely when the would-be founders heard that their organizing such a society would preclude them from receiving poor relief.

The passing of the Poor Law Amendment Act in 1834 was followed by a rapid increase in the savings bank deposits and in the membership of friendly societies; and only a few years ago, in 1891, Mr. Bland Garland, in speaking of the Bradfield Union, Berkshire, England, shows that an improved system of poor relief had the result of increasing in nineteen years the membership of the friendly societies 150 per cent, and that of doctors clubs, 148 per cent.

The societies must have a healthy atmosphere if they are to flourish, and must be free from any artificial stimulus.

The early societies suffered not only from the badly constructed poor laws, but also from the patronage of the richer classes; and here again it was proved, as Mr. Bosanquet says, that the patronized friendly societies did not fare as well as those that were entirely dependent on the members. For the organization of a friendly society must be on a democratic basis, if it be founded to last and to do good work. Its success will depend exclusively on the integrity, the coöperation, and the business ability of its members. If there be any class distinctions or ulterior aid, the undermining of the society will begin, and the result will be, necessarily, a collapse, partial or entire.

Though legislation did little to help the friendly societies between the years 1834–1870, and much to hinder their growth prior to that period, the Friendly Societies Act of 1875–1876 put the societies on a firm basis. The royal commission that formed the law, the chairman of which was Sir Stafford Northcote (Lord Iddesleigh), gave four years of hard work to their task. In 1846 the office of registrar had been made permanent, but according to the new law there was to be a registrar-in-chief with three assistants (one each for England, Scotland, and Ireland), instead of a separate registrar for each country. Yearly audits are required by the law, and a quinquennial valuation of the assets and the liabilities of each society, as well as the appointment of public auditors and valuers for the use of such societies as do not employ competent men to investigate their financial status. Provision is made to secure for members a knowledge of their rights and obligations, so that if a certain proportion of the membership of a society apply for an inspection of its affairs or for a special meeting of its members, the registrar is empowered to see that such investigation be made or such action taken as is called for.

The friendly societies that are to be mentioned belong to the two great classes — the affiliated and the centralized. In the affiliated orders the management of the lodges is independent of the federal body, they being subject only to certain general rules, and holding their own sick funds, and, as a rule, their own funeral funds as well. The lodges within a given area unite to form a district, which is composed of delegates from the branches, who meet at stated intervals to carry out the laws of the general body. The whole order is governed by a parliament of delegates from the districts, and these delegates are elected annually or biennially, and, as a body, are empowered to revise the rules of the order and to levy assessments. The parliament elects the central board of government, which consists of a president, a vice-president, a permanent secretary, the ex-president, and a board of six to nine directors. Each lodge has its own board of trustees, and its own paid secretary and visitor, the duties

of the latter being to carry the benefits to the
sick members. The district acts as a court of
arbitration for the lodges, and appoints auditors
to examine the financial status of each. The
cost of its management is met by the several
lodges. In case of unusual pressure the district or the local lodge may receive help from
the central body, but the expectation is that
each lodge shall be independent of any outside
financial aid.

The benefits consist of weekly allowances
during sickness, annuities to widows and or-
phans, funeral benefits for dead members, travelling expenses for out-of-work members in
search of employment, and in some lodges
insurance against accident and loss of tools by
fire, and the providing of convalescent homes
for the use of members recovering from pro-
tracted illness.

The centralized societies differ from the affiliated in that their chief characteristic is, as their
name implies, centralization. There is but one
benefit fund, and the contributions are received
as well as distributed from the central office.
These orders are less social than their great

rivals, as their members are not brought into as close relationship with each other.

The Independent Order of Oddfellows, Manchester Unity, the richest of the friendly societies, was founded in 1812, and is an offshoot of the Union Order of Oddfellows founded in 1745. This society was peculiarly fortunate in having for many years as its corresponding secretary, Mr. Henry Ratcliffe, who, in 1850, published his first edition of "Observation on the Rate of Mortality and Sickness existing amongst Friendly Societies." His second actuarial treatise was published in 1862, and these treatises were most valuable in showing the status of the society, and in pointing the way to make its financial condition sound.

The Unity is strengthened each year by having on an average 4613 members transferred to it from its juvenile branches. January, 1898, the adult male membership numbered 787,962; widows subscribing for funeral benefits, 10,950; juvenile members, 110,906; honorary members, 11,741; and female members, 3551; making the large total of 925,110. At the same date there were for the juvenile members, 1662

societies; and for the female, 72 lodges.   During the year 1897, 7689 were transferred from
the juvenile to the adult lodges.

The president of the society is known as the
noble grand master, and he receives a salary
of £25 a year.   The whole government is centred in the annual movable committee, which
elects the central board.   In the board is
vested the right to act as supreme court of
appeal, for it has the legal right to settle and
arbitrate any disputes that may occur in the
districts or the lodges.

The objects of the society are the payment
of a sum of money at the death of a member's
wife, the relief of members in sickness or old
age, temporary help to the widows or the children of dead members, and to members that
are travelling in search of employment.

The age limit for new members is forty-five,
and contributions are graduated according to
the age of the member at the time of his
initiation.

There are different grades of benefits, but
by a monthly payment of from 1s. 2d. to 2s.
6d. (according to age) benefits to the amount

of 8*s*. a week for full sick pay, and 4*s*. for half sick pay, £8 at death for beneficiaries of members, and £4 at death of a member's wife, are granted. The highest grade benefits are 20*s*. for full sick pay, and £20 at death of members. The contributions for such benefits are, of course, proportionally large.[1]

The monthly contributions of juveniles vary from 8½*d*. at one year of age to 1*s*. 2*d*. at fifteen, the death benefits from £2 10*s*. to £10. Sick benefits are first granted at ten years of age.

During 1897 the number of seceding members was 22,072, a slightly lower number than for the four preceding years. The grand master proposed in his annual address for 1897 that the society continue to battle with the evil of secession by "assisting in every way the real deserving cases from the Benevolent Funds of our Lodges, and in other friendly arrangements well known to and fully appreciated by all ardent Lodge and District Workers." Great stress is in fact laid on the necessity of aid-

[1] For summary of receipts and expenditures, see Appendix, Table V.

ing members who through unavoidable misfortunes are prevented from keeping up their
dues.

The Hearts of Oak benefit society, the
largest of the centralized orders, was organized in 1842. This society conducts business
with its branches through the medium of the
mail and not by local agents, and for this reason it does not come into as close relationship
with its members as do the affiliated orders.
The management has been very economic, the
expenses for the last ten years having aver-
aged but "a little over five per cent on the
gross annual income."

In addition to granting sick relief and death
benefits, the society offers a benefit of £1 10s.
to a member on the birth of a child, and medical attendance in case of sickness, a small
extra fee being paid for the last mentioned
service. A convalescent home benefit fund
has been created, and to it each member is
required to pay 1d. a quarter. The home may
be used by a member that is in need of
change of air.

The age limit for admission to membership

o

is thirty years, being lower than that of the affiliated societies because the contributions are not graduated. The regular subscription is 7s. a quarter, but this sum is increased to about 10s. by the special assessments that are levied. The sick benefits are 18s. a week for the first twenty-six weeks of sickness, half pay for a succeeding twenty-six weeks, and a weekly pension of 4s. if the illness become chronic.

Death benefits are £20 for a member, £10 for a member's wife. The society has had difficulty in checking the abuse of its membership by those who claim sick benefits unjustifiably, but the evils of malingering are being carefully guarded against by the managers.

The membership has been principally confined to the classes of professional men and skilled laborers, not reaching the workingmen as do the affiliated orders. The number of members at the end of 1897 was 220,896.[1]

The independent organization of friendly societies of women has not been as a rule very successful, women having lacked in their

[1] For receipts and expenditures, see Appendix, Table VI.

tentative efforts a knowledge of sound financial principles and of the right methods of organization.   It is hoped, however, that some of the societies which have been started will be successful, and that they may receive from the men's friendlies more generous treatment than was meted to organizations of women in the past, when the Manchester Unity could forbid its members on penalty of suspension for six months to assist any secret society of women or to attend its meetings.

From their long years of experience and in spite of their many failures, the English friendly societies have gained so honorable a position that it is possible for careful students of philanthropic problems to speak of them as an "institution of which the whole country is justly proud," and as the "backbone of provident habits."   The English societies are fortunate in that the large affiliated and centralized orders have met yearly in London since 1887 to confer on subjects of common interest,[1] and it is of incalculable advantage to

[1] The last National Conference of Friendly Societies was held in London, on January 21, 1898.   It was shown that the

them as a body and to their members as individuals, that the registrar is required to make
to Parliament an annual report of their financial
standing. Such a report is not infallible, but
it is a great safeguard against abuse to have
the societies appreciate that a yearly report
is to be made of their condition.

The large societies have a decided advantage
over the small ones in that the proportional
cost of management is much less great. A
more vital distinction is, however, that their
solvency is more assured, and that they have,
through experience, learned how best to divide
their resources. A man may, also, take reasonable pride in belonging to a large society, and
in the affiliated orders may enjoy the benefits
and privileges of being united with a vast,
widespreading body, and yet have the social
freedom that comes from being connected with a
lodge or court, the membership of which is practically limited to his immediate neighborhood.

Total adult membership was	2,958,723
The amount of capital	£22,075,895
Number of juvenile members	474,862
Amount of capital	£447,685

A further advantage that the large societies have is that they yearly add to their membership by absorbing young men advanced from the juvenile branches. These recruits have not only the merit of youth but training in economic habits.

A society to be successful, and faithfully to discharge its two chief functions of granting adequate sick relief and death benefits, must be most judicious in its choice of members and in its levying of contributions. It is essential that contributions should be graduated according to the age of the member at entering, and that records should be kept of the sickness and of the mortality of the membership. Each society can benefit by the common experience, but each should keep its own records, so that, in a different locality and under varying conditions, it may have its own data from which to estimate its liability. A careful valuation of the financial condition of the society must be made by experienced actuaries, and if the liabilities, present and prospective, be found to exceed the assets, immediate measures should be taken to change the balance.

Vigilance has to be the watchword of the societies, and even at present the need is being felt in England of carefully graduating contributions so as to make them equal the total outlay. Either the benefits must be lessened or the contributions increased, or both remedies resorted to, for the young member must be protected against having to carry the dead weight of an older membership, which has not borne its proportion of the cost of insurance.

Each society should carefully protect its members by refusing to admit any candidate that has not been able to get a doctor's certificate, by carefully supervising all claims for sick benefits, and by limiting the age of admission. Care should be taken to prevent lapsing, for though the accumulated dues of a seceding member become the property of the lodge, the real prosperity of a society must depend on the personal reliability of its members, as well as on the good faith of the management and its courage in applying sound business methods.

It has been the experience in England that fraud has not been more common in these societies than in the ordinary commercial and industrial enterprises, because they are usually managed with "rectitude, ability, and success."[1]

In the United States the fraternal societies may likewise broadly be divided into two classes: the assessment life insurance orders without branches, and those with lodges. In the last annual report of the Massachusetts Commissioner of Insurance, the statistics of 317 fraternal beneficiary associations are given. These associations started with the theory that new blood will constantly tend to keep the cost of membership low, and that assess-

[1] Table to show to what extent the savings of the English working classes are intrusted to their own associations: —

Societies under the Friendly Societies Act	No. of Societies	No. of returns	No. of members	Amount of funds
Friendly Societies (not collecting)	28,384	23,998	4,203,601	£22,695,039
Collecting Societies . .	47	43	3,875,446	2,713,214
Other Societies	21,111	557	241,446	594,808
Building Societies . . .	2,694	2,382	587,856	51,546,007
Coöperative Societies .	1,810	1,597	1,136,907	18,915,793
Trades Unions	590	401	986,817	1,515,319

"Problem of the Aged Poor," Drage, p. 300, based on Report of the Chief Registrar of Friendly Societies, year 1892; "Mutual Thrift," Rev. Frome Wilkinson; "Associations of Workingmen," Baernreither, are valuable as giving extended accounts of the friendly societies movement.

ments need not, therefore, increase in frequency or amount as the years roll on. This argument has been found to be fallacious, and though specious watchwords such as, "Pay as you go," and "Keep your reserve in your pocket," deceived many in the halcyon days of the orders, the societies, as the members have grown older, have learned to appreciate that the real cost of insurance must ultimately be paid. As the death rate grows heavy the lapses become more frequent, and the individual who retains his membership is made to meet an assessment that is too great a tax to be borne.

Many of the orders made tables of rates at haphazard and trusted to luck that the future would furnish a sufficient revenue to meet the liabilities; other societies based ·their assessments on the natural premium plan, by which system each member carries his own life insurance, the rate of premiums increasing as he grows older. When he reaches the age of fifty or sixty years, the payments become level and the younger members are then made to share the risks of his insurance. A third class based their assessments on mortality tables, and made the premiums level so that a man in the early years of his membership should meet the actuarial cost of his insurance. During the years when the current cost is less than the actual, a reserve is being accumulated, which can be drawn on when the time of greatest mortality is reached.

The best societies are now admitting that the last plan is the soundest. They feel that they have proceeded on wrong lines, and have caused their " existence to be threatened by not creating at the beginning " a reserve fund.

The liability must increase as the orders become older, for the incoming members do not contribute sufficient to meet the demands made by the heavy death rate. In the Appendix is given a table [1] showing the increase in the death rate, and in the cost of insurance of two large societies. Their experience is very similar to that of other of the great fraternals, "which have gone on constantly from their inception increasing by greater and greater strides yearly in accessions to membership, but

[1] Table VII.

as steadily and constantly is the cost of their insurance creeping upward." [1]

"What are you going to do about it?" is the grave question that the societies must ask of each other, and an answer comes from the National Fraternal Congress, which at its eleventh annual meeting, held in October, 1897, reaffirmed a resolution adopted at its preceding meeting. This resolution declared that it is the imperative duty of the orders to adjust their contributions so that they may be equitably proportioned to the risks.

The sooner the fraternals meet the question and close their ears to the siren's call — cheap insurance — the better. Cheap insurance is a delusion, for the cost of the death benefits must be met finally. The present should, by graduated payments based on a level premium plan, accumulate a reserve fund for the demands of the future. Such a system has been found essential in the English friendlies, for it not only gives "firmness and stability," but permits the "insured to continue his contract

[1] Forty-second Massachusetts Life Insurance Report, 1897, p. xx.

to the very end without any need of the increase of his rates."

The readjustment of rates is not easy, and requires courage. But unless a strong reserve fund be established by the orders, they will be found to be insolvent when the demands on them are most insistent.

The great fraternal societies, which like the Masons and the Odd Fellows number each more than three-quarters of a million of members, the Ancient Order of United Workmen with nearly four hundred thousand, and the Royal Arcanum with nearly two hundred thousand, are doing valuable work, but they must face the situation. They must in their calculations eliminate chance, so that each man, who through self-denial has accumulated savings in order to become a member of an order, may be assured of receiving a promised benefit, and need not fear that he will be called on to furnish increased contributions.

There is no questioning the importance of the workingman's providing himself by a reasonable insurance against the casualties of life, and no charity worker can fail to realize the importance of encouraging those he works amongst to join some society that will assure adequate relief in times of sickness and of death.

Each society must, however, be judged according to its merits or demerits. A friendly visitor should learn what is the financial condition of the one in which the head of her family is or should be insured, so that she may advise whether continuing to pay dues and assessments will mean throwing good money after bad.

CHAPTER IX

CONCLUDING REMARKS

WE have been accused recently of being as a people superbly indifferent to pecuniary details. If this accusation be a true one, we should individually strive to overcome the evil tendencies that have been implanted in us by the ease with which wealth has been acquired in this young country. Every effort should be made to organize self-help, by developing mutual savings agencies, that thereby, individually, we may be taught to be thrifty and provident.

The difficulty of getting volunteer service has often seemed to be an insuperable difficulty to the well-to-do when they have thought of founding workingmen's associations, but the experience of friendly societies and of building and loan associations proves that human nature is the same in all classes of society, and that prominence, influence, power, are charms that can tempt the workingman as well as the capitalist to give time and energy to organizations that can offer such rewards.

That it is true that "benevolence is in the air" is sufficient reason for great care being taken to make the air breathed by the poor more healthful because of the spirit of benevolence that has become one of its constituents. Social settlements and associated charities, training schools and child-saving agencies, are doing valuable work in teaching the poorer classes how to utilize their inherent forces. They should never, however, lose sight of the fact that whatever is organized to promote thrift must be based on sound economic principles, and be conducted in a businesslike manner. But social and philanthropic workers have not to deal only with new undertakings; they must make use chiefly of what already exists. If organized charities would appoint permanent committees to make a study of the various provident schemes that are already founded in any given locality, and to report from time to time which agencies are reliable and which are unsound, and what redress might be got by a poor man in case of usurious charges on the part of loan associations and instalment and chattel mortgage companies, most valuable assistance could be rendered by friendly visitors to the families and the individuals they are trying to assist. Such a directory of associations for promoting thrift could be a valuable guide to an inexperienced visitor.

At the risk of insistence, it must be repeated that whatever is done should be with an understanding of the conditions that surround the people who are to be aided. The charity worker can never repeat too often the forceful words: "If we have been accessory to shaking any one's sense of the duty of forethought, their feeling of parental or filial responsibility, or their conviction that if they are to live they must fit themselves for civilized life, or if we have trained any one to think that the world is a lottery and that the only rule is to rely on chance or Providence without intelligent prospect or retrospect, then we have done them as real and material and disastrous a mischief as if we had given them phosphorous necrosis in our factory, or poisoned them with sewer gas, or cheated them of their wages."[1]

May the charity worker help the poor man to acquire a "blameless and unfraudful" competence, not by a sacrifice of manliness, or by a gift, but as the reward of his own exertions. Through the exercise of frugality and forethought may the toiler be enabled to save for the future need which is greater than the need of the present; and may the reward of his thrift be a knowledge of the value of money, a relishing of the fruits of independence, and the power to enjoy life more abundantly.

[1] "Aspects of the Social Problem," p. 117.

APPENDIX

TABLE I

Tables of Rates for Policies issued in the Industrial Department of one of the large Life Insurance Companies

INCREASING LIFE AND ENDOWMENT TABLE OF RATES

Under this table the amount of insurance for the first three years appears in the column headed "minimum amount." Each year thereafter the insurance is increased by an amount equal to TEN TIMES THE WEEKLY PREMIUM. At the expiration of the period given in column headed "Endowment Term" the "maximum amount" is paid to the insured.

ONE-FOURTH only of the amount of Insurance payable if death occur within six calendar months from date of Policy; ONE-HALF only if death occur after six calendar months and within one year; and the FULL AMOUNT only if death occur after one year.

Age next Birthday	5c		10c		15c		20c		25c		30c		35c		40c		45c		50c		55c		60c		Endowment Term Years
	Min.	Max.	Min.	Max.	Min.	Max.	Min.	Max.	Min.	Max.	Min.	Max.	Min.	Max.	Min.	Max.	Min.	Max.	Min.	Max.	Min.	Max.	Min.	Max.	
10	115	148.50	230	297																					70
11	110	143	220	286																					69
12	105	137.50	210	275	315	412.50																			68
13	100	132	200	264	300	396	400	528																	67
14	96	127.50	192	255	288	382.50	384	510																	66
15	92	123	184	246	276	369	368	492	460	615															65
16	88	118.50	176	237	264	355.50	352	474	440	592.50															64
17	85	115	170	230	255	345	340	460	425	575	510	690													63
18	82	111.50	164	223	246	334.50	328	446	410	557.50	492	669	574	780.50											62
19	80	109	160	218	240	327	320	436	400	545	480	654	560	763	640	872									61
20	77	105.50	154	211	231	316.50	308	422	385	527.50	462	633	539	738.50	616	844	693	949.50							60
21	75	103	150	206	225	309	300	412	375	515	450	618	525	721	600	824	675	927	750	1030	825	1133			59
22	73	100.50	146	201	219	301.50	292	402	365	502.50	438	603	511	703.50	584	804	657	904.50	730	1005	803	1105.50			58
23	71	98	142	196	213	294	284	392	355	490	426	588	497	686	568	784	639	882	710	980	781	1078	876	1206	57
24	69	95.50	138	191	207	286.50	276	382	345	477.50	414	573	483	668.50	552	764	621	859.50	690	955	759	1050.50	852	1176	56
25	68	94	136	188	204	282	272	376	340	470	408	564	476	658	544	752	612	846	680	940	748	1034	828	1146	55
26	66	91.50	132	183	198	274.50	264	366	330	457.50	396	549	462	640.50	528	732	594	823.50	660	915	726	1006.50	816	1128	54
27	65	90	130	180	195	270	260	360	325	450	390	540	455	630	520	720	585	810	650	900	715	990	780	1080	53
28	63	87.50	126	175	189	262.50	252	350	315	437.50	378	525	441	612.50	504	700	567	787.50	630	875	693	962.50	756	1050	52
29	61	85	122	170	183	255	244	340	305	425	366	510	427	595	488	680	549	765	610	850	671	935	732	1020	51

No.																									No.
30	1002	720	660	918.50	835	600	540	751.50	480	668	420	584.50	360	501	300	417.50	240	334	180	250.50	120	167	83.50	60	50
31	972	696	638	891	810	580	522	729	464	648	406	567	348	486	290	405	232	324	174	243	116	162	81	58	49
32	954	684	627	874.50	795	570	513	715.50	456	636	399	556	342	477	285	397.50	228	318	171	238.50	114	159	79.50	57	48
33	924	660	605	847	770	550	495	693	440	616	385	539	330	462	275	385	220	308	165	231	110	154	77	55	47
34	906	648	594	830.50	755	540	486	679.50	432	604	378	528.50	324	453	270	377.50	216	302	162	226.50	108	151	75.50	54	46
35	876	624	572	803	730	520	468	657	416	584	364	517	312	438	260	365	208	292	156	219	104	146	73	52	45
36	858	612	561	786.50	715	510	459	643.50	408	572	357	500.50	306	429	255	357.50	204	286	153	214.50	102	143	71.50	51	44
37	828	588	539	759	690	490	441	621	392	552	343	483	294	414	245	345	196	276	147	207	98	138	69	49	43
38	810	576	528	742.50	675	480	432	607.50	384	540	336	472.50	288	405	240	337.50	192	270	144	202.50	96	135	67.50	48	42
39	780	552	506	715	650	460	414	585	368	520	322	455	276	390	230	325	184	260	138	195	92	130	65	46	41
40	762	540	495	698.50	635	450	405	571.50	360	508	315	444.50	270	381	225	317.50	180	254	135	190.50	90	127	63.50	45	40
41	732	516	473	671	610	430	387	549	344	488	301	427	258	366	215	305	172	244	129	183	86	122	61	43	39
42	714	504	462	654.50	595	420	378	535.50	336	476	294	416.50	252	357	210	297.50	168	238	126	178.50	84	119	59.50	42	38
43	684	480	440	627	570	400	360	513	320	456	280	399	240	342	200	285	160	228	120	171	80	114	57	40	37
44	666	468	429	610.50	555	399	351	499.50	312	444	273	388	234	333	195	277.50	156	222	117	166.50	78	111	55.50	39	36
45	636	444	407	583	530	370	333	477	288	424	259	371	222	318	185	265	148	206	111	159	74	106	53	37	35
46	618	432	396	566.50	515	360	324	463.50	324	412	252	363.50	216	309	180	257.50	144	206	108	154.50	72	103	51.50	36	34
47	600	420	385	550	500	350	315	450	280	400	245	350	210	300	175	250	140	200	105	150	70	100	50	35	33
48	570	396	363	522.50	475	330	297	427.50	264	380	231	333.50	198	285	165	237.50	132	190	99	142.50	66	94	47.50	33	32
49	552	384	352	506	450	330	288	414	256	368	224	322	192	276	160	230	128	184	96	138	64	92	46	32	31
50	534	372	341	489.50	445	310	279	400.50	248	356	217	311.50	186	267	155	222.50	124	178	93	133.50	62	89	44.50	31	30
51	504	348	319	462	420	290	261	378	232	336	203	294	174	252	145	203	116	168	87	126	58	84	42	29	29
52	486	336	308	445.50	405	280	252	364.50	224	324	196	283.50	162	243	140	202.50	112	162	84	121.50	56	81	40.50	28	28
53	468	324	297	429	390	270	243	351	216	312	189	273	156	234	135	195	108	156	78	117	54	78	39	27	27
54	450	312	286	412.50	375	260	234	337.50	208	300	182	262.50	150	225	130	187.50	104	150	78	112.50	52	75	37.50	26	26
55	432	300	275	396	360	250	225	324	200	288	175	252	144	216	125	180	100	144	75	108	50	72	36	25	25
56	414	288	264	379.50	345	240	216	310.50	192	276	168	241.50	138	207	120	172.50	96	138	72	103.50	48	69	34.50	24	24
57	384	264	242	352	320	220	198	288	176	256	154	224	128	192	110	160	88	128	66	96	44	64	32	22	23
58	366	252	231	335.50	305	210	189	274.50	168	244	147	213	122	183	105	152.50	84	122	63	91.50	42	61	30.50	21	22
59	348	240	220	319	290	200	180	261	160	232	140	203	116	174	100	145	80	116	60	87	40	58	29	20	21
60	330	228	209	302	275	190	171	247.50	152	220	133	192.50	110	165	95	137.50	76	110	57	82.50	38	55	27.50	19	20
61	312	216	198	286	260	180	162	234	144	208	126	182	104	156	90	130	72	104	54	78	36	52	26	18	19
62	294	204	187	269.50	245	170	153	220.50	136	196	119	171.50	98	147	85	122.50	68	98	51	73.50	34	49	24.50	17	18
63	276	192	176	253	230	160	144	207	128	184	112	161	92	138	80	115	64	92	48	69	32	46	23	16	17
64	258	180	165	236.50	215	150	135	193.50	120	172	105	150.50	86	129	75	107.50	60	86	45	64.50	30	43	21.50	15	16
65	240	168	154	220	200	140	126	180	112	160	98	140	80	120	70	100	56	80	42	60	28	40	20	14	15
66	222	156	143	203.50	185	130	117	166.50	104	148	91	129.50	74	111	65	92.50	52	74	39	55.50	26	37	18.50	13	14
67	216	156	132	198	180	130	108	162	96	144	84	126	72	108	60	90	48	72	36	54	24	36	18	13	13
68	198	144	121	181.50	165	120	99	148.50	88	132	77	115.50	66	99	55	82.50	44	66	33	49.50	22	33	16.50	12	12
69	180	132	121	181.50	150	110	90	135	80	120	66	105	60	90	50	75	44	60	33	45	20	30	15	11	11
70	162	120	110	148.50	135	100	90	121.50	80	108	70	94.50	60	81	50	67.50	40	54	30	40.50	20	27	13.50	10	10

TABLE II

Infantile Endowment Table of Rates for 1898

BASED ON A WEEKLY PREMIUM OF 10 CENTS

AMOUNT PAYABLE IF DEATH OCCUR DURING THE FOLLOWING PERIODS

Age next Birthday.	Under 3 mo.	Under 6 mo.	Under 9 mo.	Under 1 year.	2d year.	3d year.	4th year.	5th year.	6th year.	7th year.	8th year.	9th year.
2	16	20	24	30	34	40	48	58	110	160	200	240
3	18	22	28	34	40	48	58	102	150	200	240	
4	20	26	32	40	48	58	94	140	200	240		
5	22	28	36	48	58	86	130	190	240			
6	24	32	44	58	78	120	180	240				
7	28	38	52	70	110	170	240					
8	32	44	70	100	160	240						
9	40	56	100	150	240							

On each anniversary of the Policy, after the Insured reaches twelve years of age, there will be added to the maximum amount named in the above table, ONE DOLLAR.

The Endowment period and the amount payable at the end of such period are as follows: —

Policies issued at age 2 mature in 47 yr. for $276.00
"   "   " 3   "   48   "   278.00
"   "   " 4   "   49   "   280.00
"   "   " 5   "   51   "   283.00
"   "   " 6   "   53   "   286.00
"   "   " 7   "   56   "   290.00
"   "   " 8   "   62   "   297.00
"   "   " 9   "   68   "   304.00

For 5 cents per week the benefits are one-half those named above.

No higher premium than 10 cents will be taken.

TABLE III

In an address before the Massachusetts Legislature in 1895, an official of one of the large industrial insurance companies gave an analysis of the disposition by his company of its total income. He has furnished, by request, an analysis for the five years 1891–1896, inclusive. He gives the following percentages of the disposition of the total income from the industrial business of his company : —

Paid policy holders	34.67
Increase in reserve	15.94
Commissions for collections	14.23
Commissions for procurement of new business . . .	3.15
Excess of commissions paid arising out of lapses[1] . .	6.50
Expenses[2] for medical examinations, taxes, licenses, rents, printing, stationery, advertising, furniture and fixtures, travelling expenses, postage, expressage, salaries, and dividends to stockholders[3]	21.57
Surplus put to credit of policy holders, part of which has been paid to them in cash in 1897	3.94
	100.00

[1] The company actually lost in money from lapses in the year 1896.

[2] A part of this expense was caused by lapses.

[3] Dividends paid to stockholders are limited by law to seven per cent on the capital of $2,000,000.

TABLE IV

Table of Rates for Policies issued in the Ordinary Life Insurance Department of one of the large Industrial Companies.

PREMIUMS FOR AN INSURANCE OF $500.00, PAYABLE AT DEATH

Age nearest Birthday.	Annual.	Semi-Annual.	Quar-terly.	All Policies issued through the Intermediate Branch will be for $500, premiums payable annually, semi-annually, or quarterly. Applications may, however, be taken for multiples of $500, such as $1000 or $1500, in which case, instead of issuing one Policy for the full amount, $500 Policies will be issued up to the amount of the application, but in such case only one application is to be written.
18	$10 35	$5.38	$2.74	
19	10.70	5.56	2.83	
20	11.04	5.74	2.92	
21	11.35	5.90	3.01	
22	11.66	6.06	3.09	
23	11.96	6.22	3.17	
24	12.26	6.38	3 25	
25	12.56	6.53	3.33	
26	12.87	6.69	3.41	
27	13.17	6.85	3.49	
28	13.50	7.02	3.58	
29	13.84	7.20	3.67	
30	14.19	7.38	3.76	
31	14.56	7.57	3.86	
32	14.95	7.77	3.96	
33	15.36	7.99	4 07	**Paid-up**
34	15.79	8.21	4.19	
35	16.25	8.45	4.31	A non-participating paid-up Policy, payable in the same manner as the original Policy, will be granted for the amount specified in the following tables of paid-up values, after the premiums for three full years shall have been paid, and the Policy satisfactorily released and surrendered therefor to the Company at the Home Office while in force, or within six months from default of payment of any premium.
36	16.74	8.70	4.43	
37	17.25	8.97	4.57	
38	17.79	9.25	4.71	
39	18.36	9.55	4.86	
40	18.96	9.86	5.02	
41	19.60	10 19	5.19	
42	20.28	10.54	5.37	
43	20.99	10.91	5 56	
44	21.75	11.31	5.76	
45	22.55	11.72	5.98	
46	23.40	12.17	6.20	
47	24.30	12.63	6.44	
48	25.25	13.13	6.69	
49	26.26	13.65	6 96	
50	27.33	14.21	7 24	
51	28.47	14.80	7.54	
52	29 68	15.43	7.86	
53	30.96	16.10	8 20	
54	32.32	16.81	8.56	
55	33.77	17.56	8 95	**Loans on Policies**
56	35 30	18 36	9.36	
57	36.94	19 21	9.79	The Company will loan money on policies, at six per cent interest, payable annually, in advance, upon receiving satisfactory assignment of the Policies as collateral security while in force.
58	38.68	20.11	10.25	
59	40.53	21.08	10.74	
60	42.51	22.10	11.26	
61	44.61	23.20	11.82	
62	46.85	24.36	12.41	
63	49.23	25.60	13.05	
64	51.78	26.92	13.72	
65	54 49	28.33	14.44	

TABLE V

Receipts and Expenditures of the Independent Order of Oddfellows, Manchester Unity

SUMMARY OF RECEIPTS AND EXPENDITURE of the several Funds belonging to the Unity, for the year ending 31st December, 1896.

Description of Fund.	Received for Contributions, Interest, Entrance Fees, etc.			Paid on Account of Members for Sick and Funeral Benefits, Management, etc.		
	£	s.	d.	£	s.	d.
Sick and Funeral Funds	1,181,208	3	10	792,275	6	11
Management Funds of Lodges .	304,233	16	3	308,995	8	2
Widow and Orphan Societies . .	46,345	18	3	34,634	11	2
Past Grand Lodges	2,095	2	11	1,490	1	10
Juvenile Societies	38,810	18	7	30,804	5	1
Benevolent or other Funds . . .	14,217	18	0	13,844	3	7
Total	1,586,911	17	10	1,182,043	16	9

Increase on the Year . . . . £388,932 16s. 1d.

SUMMARY OF CAPITAL

Description of Fund.	31st December, 1896		
	£	s.	d
Sick and Funeral Funds of Lodges	8,302,389	13	0
District Funeral Funds	364,524	8	8
Management Funds of Lodges	113,640	6	4
Management Funds of Districts	7,918	0	0
Widow and Orphan Societies	431,939	17	3
Past Grands Lodges	11,675	7	6
Juvenile Societies	116,899	10	8
Benevolent or other Funds	50,028	4	8
Total Capital of the Unity	9,399,015	8	1

TABLE VI

Hearts of Oak Benefit Society. Statistics taken from 56th Annual Statement

"After deducting £3552 18s. 3d. levied for the Convalescent Home Fund, the following is a concise comparison of the past two years' receipts and expenditure : —

TABLE SHOWING RECEIPTS AND EXPENDITURES FOR 1896 AND 1897

	1896.		1897.	
	Amount.	Ratio.	Amount.	Ratio.
	£ s. d.		£ s. d.	
Gross Receipts	472,000 14 10	100.00	491,226 0 0	100.00
Claims Paid	309,654 3 6	65.00	328,256 12 7	66.82
	162,346 11 4	34.40	162,969 7 5	33.18
Expenses of Management . . .	27,242 9 7	5.77	26,366 5 1	5.37
	135,104 1 9	28.63	136,603 2 4	27.81
Postages and Emblems charged again to Members	1,574 13 2	.33	1,655 17 6	.34
Amount added to Reserve Fund .	133,529 8 7	28.30	134,947 4 10	27.47

From this statement it appears that of every £100 of the Gross Income, £66 16s. 5d. was paid away in satisfaction of Claims, £5 7s. 5d. was required for Management Expenses, 6s. 9d. for Postages, etc. (chargeable to Members individually), leaving £27 9s. 5d. for transfer to the Reserve Fund."

Summary of Claims Paid by the Hearts of Oak Society for the undermentioned Benefits, from the Commencement of the Institution, June 20th, 1842, to December 31st, 1897.

Sickness and Superannuation	£3,247,564	16	8
Lying-in Claims	865,843	10	0
Members' Funerals } Members' Wives' Funerals }	687,350	15	5
Loss by Fire	33,174	19	4
Sold Out Cases	21,697	7	4
Imprisonment	198	13	4
Total	£4,855,830	2	1

TABLE SHOWING STEADY GROWTH OF THE SOCIETY

Year.	Number of Members.	Reserve Fund.
1866	12,051	£44,386
1868	15,903	54,526
1870	21,484	67,321
1872	32,837	93,840
1874	51,144	145,556
1875	64,421	179,995
1876	76,369	223,780
1878	90,603	326,640
1880	93,615	437,772
1882	98,873	559,327
1884	105,268	696,206
1885	108,685	766,350

TABLE VII

KNIGHTS OF HONOR (founded, 1876)

Year.	Mortuary Assessments.	Claims Paid.	Members admitted in year.	Members at End of Year.	Deaths Occurring.	Lapses.	Death Rate per 1000 Members.	Average Cost to Each Member.
1896	$4,261,084	$4,155,004	8,358	96,633	2,137	24,800	20 2	$40 23
1895	4,058,331	3,944,233	8,836	115,212	2,067	11,342	17.6	34.54
1894	3,844,550	3,845,117	9,151	119,785	1,972	10,748	16 4	32.61
1893	4,020,074	4,017,486	9,321	123,354	2,062	10,978	16.5	32.11
1892	4,279,401	4,283,392	8,297	127,073	2,051	11,672	15.8	32.97
1891	4,209,046	4,207,500	11,282	132,499	2,081	11,914	15.5	31.43
1890	3,483,982	3,482,000	12,062	135,212	1,946	6,657	14.6	26.10
1889	3,415,555	3,421,033	12,552	131,753	1,740	4,476	13 5	26.56
1888	3,198,137	3,210,656	11,025	125,417	1,696	6,824	13.7	25.75
1887	3,178,435	3,175,400	8,861	122,912	1,607	10,511	12.9	25.52
1886	3,080,919	3,080,600	8,803	126,169	1,510	6,619	12.0	24.49
1885	2,999,060	3,079,000	8,982	125,495	1,487	10,601	11.7	23.61
1884	2,709,562	2,634,251	10,640	128,601	1,426	8,922	11.1	21.09
1883	2,856,617	3,028,000	12,776	128,309	1,427	8,566	11.2	22.51

ROYAL ARCANUM (founded, 1877)

Year.	Mortuary Assessments.	Claims Paid.	Members admitted in year.	Members at End of Year.	Deaths Occurring.	Lapses.	Death Rate per 1000 Members.	Average Cost to Each Member.
1896	$4,882,548	$5,002,674	22,452	190,261	1,731	4,520	9.5	$26.80
1895	4,204,008	4,197,446	20,454	174,060	1,527	4,174	9.2	25.22
1894	4,190,030	3,959,600	16,975	159,307	1,344	4,750	8.7	27.23
1893	3,693,916	3,770,750	16,086	148,426	1,296	3,553	9.1	25 87
1892	3,432,834	3,401,750	17,293	137,189	1,141	3,729	8 7	26 18
1891	3,129,420	3,096,250	17,089	124,766	1,009	2,680	8.5	26.50
1890	2,803,060	2,717,302	16,802	111,366	947	2,482	9 0	26.77
1889	2,158,310	2,146,526	13,357	97,993	750	1,599	8 1	23.33
1888	2,120,609	2,024,700	10,789	86,935	690	2,335	8.3	25 53
1887	1,933,033	1,940,500	10,847	79,171	636	1,863	8.5	25.73
1886	1,543,829	1,512,000	12,010	70,823	522	1,622	7.9	23.43
1885	1,263,846	1,260,500	9,217	60,957	430	1,641	7.5	22.02
1884	1,053,103	1,042,500	7,973	53,811	380	1,526	7.5	20.73
1883	879,911	906,000	9,126	47,744	303	1,113	6.9	20.05

From the "Dilemma of Fraternal Orders." The *Spectator*, October, 1897.